THE BODYGUARD

WORTH THE WEIGHT BOOK THREE

JASON COLLINS

ACKNOWLEDGMENTS

A very special thank you to:

My cover designer, Cate Ashwood Designs.

My editor, Tanja Ongkiehong.

My proofreaders, Leonie Duncan and Shelley Chastagner.

Cover photographer Eric McKinney of 6:12 Photography.

CONTENTS

JESSE

I COULDN'T KEEP THE SMILE OFF MY FACE AS I WALKED UP THE RICKETY-looking wooden front steps of the restaurant. It was a gorgeous, bright, sunny day in the rural town of Winchester, South Carolina, and I was starved after getting in late from a series of delayed flights last night. As it turned out, flying from the star-studded hills of Holly-wood all the way to a sleepy, picturesque country town in the South was not a direct path in the slightest. I was still feeling a little groggy and jet-lagged, having traveled through several time zones to get here, but as an actor, I was used to that.

The sun was out, there wasn't a single cloud in the bright blue sky, and I could hear birds chittering and chirping in the trees, even in the parking lot of the restaurant. I considered that a pretty good sign. The only birds I ever encountered in Los Angeles were hyper aggressive seagulls that would be just as comfortable swiping a French fry right out of your mouth as they would be flying through the fires of hell. And then there were the omnipresent pigeons. And the exotic pet birds who would routinely escape from the homes of the eccentric Hollywood elite.

But here, surrounded by miles and miles of unspoiled, dense wilderness, there were real birds. The kind you might see in one of those diligently compiled bird-watching guides. But it wasn't just the avian population that felt more genuine, more down-to-earth. As I walked up onto the front dining porch of Beulah's Biscuits, I looked around at the tables filled with kind, smiling faces. There were grandparents feeding morsels of grits to their tiny, happy grandchildren. There were couples dressed in church clothes. Many of the women went without makeup, which was a rarity in Los Angeles. The fashion here was so outdated that it could nearly wrap back around and be considered vintage, except that I got the feeling fashion trends were about as relevant as Wall Street in a modest neck of the woods like Winchester.

As I glanced around, I saw a hand-painted sign that read: *PLEASE SEAT YOURSELF, SUGAR!* I smiled to myself and walked over to take an empty corner table on the side of the wraparound covered porch. It was pretty picturesque, even if it didn't bode well for my hopes of watching my waistline while here. It was all open-air except for the mosquito netting that blocked out the buzzing insects. A waitress walking by caught my eye and gave me a nod of acknowledgment.

"I'll be with you in just a minute, hon," she said with a syrupy Southern accent.

"Thanks," I replied with a smile.

Seeing an unattended menu on an empty table, I hopped up to go grab it and nearly walked straight into a gigantic, handsome guy walking by in the process. My shoulder knocked against his muscular arm, and I hurriedly swiveled around to apologize. But when he turned to look me in the eyes, the words got stuck in my throat. I stared wide-eyed and slack-jawed at the man, my whole body tingling with arousal. He was impossibly tall and broad, with bulging biceps and a no-nonsense scowl that made him look like some kind of cartoon strongman. I had no doubt in my mind this was a guy who could kick my ass without even breaking a sweat. His appearance led me to wonder if he was some kind of athlete, maybe a professional wrestler or something crazy. I worried for a moment he would interpret my clumsiness as an invitation to a fight, but I need not have worried.

The gorgeous man gave me the faintest of good-natured nods and then kept moving, leaving me to stand in the same spot, gawking after him. I couldn't believe my eyes. I had come here to this small town fully expecting not to see a single man I would be attracted to. Perhaps that was my own fault, my own biases. I had never spent much time in the South, so most of what I had to go by was, admittedly, just a bunch of stereotypes. After all, the west coast was a totally different world from this rural setting.

But the guy I had just bumped into was precisely the kind of man I would have imagined living in a place like Winchester... in my wildest, most vivid fantasies that is. I swallowed hard at the lump in my throat, my hands clasping and unclasping as I stared at the man's wide, powerful back disappearing through the door to the interior of the restaurant. He looked like he could easily bench-press my body weight, which was saying something in recent days, since I had gained a bit of weight. Like he could pick me up and pin me to a wall, his hard, thick body pushed against me so that I could feel every blisteringly hot inch of him. I could imagine those dark eyes gazing intensely into mine, sending shivers of pleasure down my spine.

What could I say? I loved a guy who looked like he might moonlight as a lumberjack, and this man certainly fit the bill. I found myself fantasizing about being locked up in a folksy wooden cottage with this mysterious stranger, the two of us pressed together in a confined space, his large hands roving down my body, manhandling me, moving and bending me to his will. I licked my lips, nearly salivating at the thought of kneeling in front of him, tugging the engorged head of his shaft between my lips, listening to him grunt and groan with satisfaction as I gave him exactly what he deserved. He had the body of a hardworking man, and I couldn't help but daydream about getting to be the one to help him unwind. Maybe I could show him how things were done on the west coast, give him a little taste of Hollywood magic.

I watched closely as the handsome guy walked through the small diner and took a seat at a booth where a middle-aged woman was sitting. I saw the light come on in the woman's eyes, crinkling into

3

crow's feet at the corners with genuine affection. As soon as the handsome man sat down, he reached across the table to briefly embrace the woman's hands. I could see the pure love and admiration in her eyes, as well as his, and for a split second, I wondered if he was dating an older woman. But when I looked a little closer, it became evident to me that she was his mother, a fact that immediately made my heart melt a little. Even though he probably outweighed her by at least a hundred pounds of muscle and she looked to be barely over five feet tall, she looked at him like he was a big, soft teddy bear. The trust and love apparent in their dynamic were impressive to me. How sweet. A southern country boy meeting up with his beloved mom for a little catch-up date at a folksy brunch restaurant. The contrast of the man's bear-like, intimidating appearance with his heartfelt reunion with his mother, who clearly adored him, was almost too much for me to handle.

It looked like something a friend of mine would have filmed for a made-for-TV feel-good movie about family and togetherness, but it wasn't for any camera or audience. It was genuine and real. If that wasn't a good sign of things to come during my little retreat from the harsh lights and judgmental culture of Los Angeles, I didn't know what was. As much as I loved the hustle and bustle of Hollywood, it could get a little tiring having to cope with the constant rat race, the insincerity of relationships, the fact that everyone was looking for a head to step on to get ahead.

There were lots of fun times to be had out on the famed west coast, but it took a lot of energy. Even a guy like me, who sometimes thrived on stress and a busy schedule, could get burned out from time to time. I was happy to be here in Winchester, where the pace of life seemed to be slowed down to half speed compared to home. Then again, I knew I'd feel comfortable here. The reason I had chosen Winchester was because my parents had taken me on a couple of road trips when I was a kid, and we had stopped in Winchester along the way. The town had been beautiful and peaceful. It had left an impression on me as a child, and I knew it was the perfect place for me to escape to as an adult. I had a good feeling I was going to like it here, especially if that handsome guy and his mom were any indication.

As I finally tore my eyes away from their adorable interaction, I did a double take. A waitress came through the back door onto the wraparound porch carrying a massive tray, balanced with several plates of delicious-looking food piled high. A veritable smorgasbord of various sweet, savory, buttery aromas wafted past my nose, and I sucked in a deep, appreciative breath.

"Wow. I want all of that," I murmured to myself, not realizing at first that I'd said the words out loud. That is, until the waitress giggled and caught my eye.

"If you want to take a seat, I'll be right with ya, darlin'," she remarked.

"Right. Yes. Of course," I said, a little flushed around the cheeks.

As she carried the tray to a table of locals dressed up after church, I slid back into my seat at the corner table and started to look at the menu. It took all my willpower not to continue stealing glances over at the handsome guy and his mother through the glossy diner window, but if there was anything on this planet most likely to distract my attention, it was the paragraph-long descriptions of menu items like *"Buttermilk Biscuits 'n' Gravy Tower with Applewood Bacon"*, or *"Swirly Cinnamon Bun Pancakes"*, or possibly my favorite: *"Beulah's Gutbuster Brunch Bonanza."* That last one made me actually pick up the menu and hold it up closer to my face, as though my eyes had to be playing a trick on me.

But nope. It was real.

My mouth watered as I read the description below. It involved southern-style cheesy grits with house-made spicy sausage gravy, a fried green tomato BLT biscuit, a side of hash browns, three eggs cooked to preference, and, almost as a final Hail Mary toward any semblance of a balanced meal, a cup of fresh fruit.

I could hardly believe what I was reading. It was easy to get caught up in the photos of food and the nearly pornographic descriptions of menu items. But luckily, I had thought ahead. Last night, while waiting for the rental car company to finish my paperwork, I had searched for local breakfast joints on my phone. Naturally, I had decided on Beulah's. And because I often had trouble deciding what to order, I had inspected the menu online beforehand. Somehow I had managed to skim past the Gut-buster, but I had already mentally selected an item amusingly named "The Six-Count of Monte Cristo," which was a deep-fried ham and jam sandwich dusted with confectioners sugar and accompanied by no less than six slices of thick-cut bacon.

It was a pun plus bacon and powdered sugar. How in the world could I say no?

Just as I set down the menu, fully secure in my decision, the waitress came over to my table with a pen nestled behind her ear and a big smile on her face. She couldn't have been any older than nineteen, fresh-faced, and friendly looking. Her name tag, to my endless enjoyment, read FLO.

"You got any questions 'bout the menu this morning?" she asked, tilting her head to one side so that her flouncy blonde ponytail bounced cheerily.

"Not about the menu, no. But I have to ask: is your name really Flo?" I chuckled.

She grinned and rolled her eyes. "Believe it or not, yep. Well, technically, it's Florence. But Flo is what I prefer. I'm Beulah's granddaughter," she replied.

"Wait, there's a real Beulah?" I asked, taken aback.

She giggled, looking at me like I was insane. "Of course there is, silly! Who else would the place be named after?" she said with a laugh. "She retired a couple years ago, but it's still my grandma's place through and through. You know, she designed the whole menu herself."

"Well, she did a great job. Everything sounds fantastic," I replied.

"Why, thank you! I'll be sure to pass that on to Grandma," she said with a wink. "Now, have you made a decision about your breakfast today, sir?"

"Mhm. I'd love to have the Monte Cristo, please," I said. "And a black coffee."

She took the pen from behind her ear and a notepad from a pocket on her apron, scribbled down my order, and then gave me another big smile. "Alrighty! I'll go put this in right away. I'll be back real soon with your coffee."

"Thank you," I said. She gave me a nod and walked away, back inside the restaurant.

As soon as she was gone, the worry began to set in. Biting my lip, I glanced down at my waistline and promptly laid out a napkin in my lap to hide some of my stomach pudge. It wasn't a massive weight gain or anything. For most people, it might not have even seemed like much of an issue. But for me it was different.

It was true what they say about the camera adding ten pounds. Unfortunately, though, my diet and exercise regimen (or rather the lack thereof) had added a good ten to fifteen on their own. In Hollywood terms, that was a big difference. People in L.A. were constantly trying to shrink themselves, always trying to be the most trim, the most chic. It could be a little toxic spending all my time in that hyperconscious world full of gossip magazines and celebrity blogs. Personally, it didn't bother me all that much except for when someone pointed it out. One might think that polite society of today would frown upon such remarks, but in Hollywood, everything a relatively famous actor like me does is under intense scrutiny.

On set, my costars were all supportive and friendly as always. After all, we had been working together for years. Soap operas functioned on a high-speed turnaround, with long days of filming and a lot of downtime on the sound stage. That meant I got to spend a lot of time chatting and bonding with my coworkers. The cast of Bannister Heights, of which I was an integral part, were all much chummier and tight-knit than we seemed on television, where soap opera rules dictated we should always be in some kind of conflict. That was what kept the show moving forward, after all: the drama. And most of the time, I loved it. Landing the role of heart-breaker Adrian Bannister was a milestone in my acting career. I wasn't quite a household name yet, but in some households where soap opera legacies reigned supreme, the name Jesse Blackwood was well known.

For diehard fans of the show, who had been following its highly dramatic plot lines for nearly a decade now, the introduction of Adrian was a big deal. I loved my job. I loved my audience. I loved my coworkers. But I had to admit that the grueling hours and constantly living under a microscope had caused me to play fast and loose with my own well-being and health.

That was why I had come here to Winchester, as an official break from acting. I needed time to relax, to get myself back into fighting condition so I could come back to the show at my best. And as I looked around at the pleasant crowd here for brunch, I felt secure in my decision. Nobody was ogling me. Nobody was trying to surreptitiously snap a photo of me with their cell phone. People weren't whispering and shooting furtive glances my way. Out here, in rural South Carolina, I could just blend into the crowd. I could be just like everybody else for once.

And then I heard it.

Click. Click-click. Flash.

My heart began to race, and my confidence plummeted. There it was. The telltale sound of a camera flashing nearby. I glanced at a spot around the corner of the restaurant, and my eyes landed on the culprit, a photographer with a big, fancy camera. I did what I always did. I turned away and tried to ignore him, though I knew my discomfort was obvious on my face. Of course I couldn't escape the paparazzi, not even way out here. They were so persistent! I should have known I would be an irresistible target for one of those slime balls.

I was just about to get up and go inside to tell the waitress to make my breakfast a to-go order when I felt a firm, large hand on my shoulder. I looked up, surprised to see that the handsome guy from earlier was standing over me, a fierce but calm look on his face. Before I could say anything, he glanced over at the paparazzo and then gave me a look that clearly indicated that he was going to take care of the issue himself.

"Wait here," he said gruffly.

"Okay," I replied in a near whisper.

He marched down the steps of the porch and right up to the camera guy, his hands curled into fists. My heart raced like crazy as I half expected a fight to break out. But then, I realized that the mysterious stranger was just giving the guy a very stern talking-to. And judging by the look of fear on the paparazzo's face, it was very effective.

The guy sheepishly handed over his camera, a feat I had never seen happen before back in L.A. My rugged hero promptly deleted the photos, gave the guy back his camera, and pointed for the guy to leave. To my complete amazement, he did as he was told. No contest. I watched with awe as the tough guy walked back to my table. I stared at him wide-eyed, barely able to think clearly. I was normally so quick and snappy, but he had truly stunned me into silence.

He gave me a self-assured nod and said in a low growl, "Sorry about that guy. He shouldn't give you any more trouble. Welcome to Winchester."

With that, he walked away back inside to his charming date with his mom. I stared after him totally dumbfounded, feeling as though there must be pink cartoon hearts flying around my head. My waitress returned to give me my mug of black coffee, and as I sat there trying to come to terms with the amazing event that had just transpired, I gazed adoringly at the man, obscured by the line of hot steam emanating from my coffee cup.

Maybe my stay in Winchester would be more exciting than I had hoped.

MARSHALL

THE WARM AIR AND SOFT CHOIR OF CRICKETS OFF IN THE DISTANCE greeted me as I stepped out of The Chisel. The glowing light from inside didn't do much to dim the twinkling stars that decorated the sky above, and it was a nice break from the bustling night inside.

It would have been a hell of a lot more pleasant of an experience if Bill weren't leaning on my shoulder, stumbling along beside me while I held him up and helped him toward the yellow cab. His eyes were glassy, and while he was never the kind of guy to put up a fight when getting escorted out of a bar, he didn't like making it easy, either. But I had an iron grip that made sure he wasn't going anywhere.

I'd handled much worse than Bill, after all.

"Woah, hold on, where are we going?" Bill asked, a little disoriented as he stepped carefully down to the gravel parking area. "Did I finish my beer? We're not fighting, are we?"

"No," I said simply.

It was a curt, potent word I had come to get a lot of use out of over the years. If you knew how to say it with just the right, firm tone, people usually assumed you knew what you were doing and that you were someone who ought to be left alone. In my book, those were two things I didn't mind one bit.

Besides, it didn't help my job to let people think I was the kind of guy who liked small talk. That was what the bartender was for. I was the bouncer here at the bar of choice for most of the town's hard-working people. At least, that was what most people figured I was. Officially, I was just a hired hand around here, and I had started out loading boxes and covering bartending shifts when Parker needed a night off. But it hadn't taken long for that to turn into being some-thing of a peacekeeper in the bar. I looked the part, and I didn't mind doing it one bit.

"He's early tonight," said Wyatt, the cab driver, as he stepped out of the driver's seat and came around to open the back door for Bill as we approached. "Didn't give you any trouble, did he?"

"No," I grunted.

I wasn't the type to brag, but I didn't think Bill could have given me trouble even if he wanted to. I had hauled the guy staggering out of The Chisel enough times to know how much muscle was under his hairy exterior, and the answer was *not that much*. He was never an angry drunk, just sloppy.

"Friend kept buying me drinks, and I must've lost track," Bill said with a chuckle.

I gave Wyatt a subtle nod behind Bill to confirm the story, and Wyatt laughed.

"Wait, this is a cab," Bill observed, furrowing his brow and staring at the vehicle thoughtfully while swaying slightly.

"That's uh… that's right, bud," Wyatt said, eyeing Bill up and down.

"I didn't call a cab," he said at last, looking at me with a genuinely confused look that told me his vision must have been swimming.

"I did," I said in a calm yet firm voice.

"Marshall's just lookin' out for you, bud," Wyatt said as my eyes moved between the two of them, wondering if we'd have to do a little persuading to get Bill to climb into the cab.

"Aw, you're just rubbin' in the damn football game," Bill said, attempting to make a waving gesture with his free hand but nearly smacking Wyatt in the chest instead.

"Never," I assured Bill as I put my hand on his head to keep him from bumping it as he bent down to get into the back seat of the cab.

Making a big deal about the high school reunion football game I helped win earlier this summer would have been the last thing to ever cross my mind, of course. I always let my actions do the talking. Bill and some of his friends had been the ones running their mouths about it leading up to the big game, and they got put in their place on the field. Had to admit, though, people were a lot better behaved around the bar after watching me play. I wasn't about to complain about that. All I had to do was keep building my muscles and let their imaginations do the work.

"Do you know what it's like getting tackled by this guy?" Bill said, turning to Wyatt with raised eyebrows and pointing at me as if I were a celebrity. "It hurts! He's like that superhero, whatshisname. The one who's real strong."

"A classic," Wyatt said, trying desperately to keep a straight face, and I couldn't hold back a crack of a smile either.

"Stay safe," I said to Bill before carefully closing the door on him and giving Wyatt a curt nod. "Thanks."

"Hey man, no problem," Wyatt said with a chuckle. "He'll regret it in the morning. You should take him with you one night next time you're looking for a date, sounds like he'd be a half-decent wingman without even trying."

I laughed faintly, then nodded to the cab.

"Make sure he settles up with you for the fare," I told Wyatt. "If he doesn't, call me."

All that meant was that if Bill was too drunk to pay his cab fare, Wyatt could call us at The Chisel in the morning, and we'd square up with him and get the money from Bill next time he came in for a drink. The important part was getting our patrons home safe, and Bill was a regular, so none of us were worried about someone running out on the tab.

"Never had to yet, but I appreciate it, Marshall," Wyatt said, waving to me as he circled back around to the driver's seat. "Y'all have a good night, all right?"

"Drive safe," I grunted, tapping the cab with my knuckle and heading back toward the door.

I rolled my shoulders back and felt a few bones pop as I stretched out my arms. I was closing tonight, so I'd be around a while longer, hopefully with fewer people to haul outside. It was rarely a problem at The Chisel. This wasn't the kind of place where fistfights broke out every weekend. But sometimes the guys got riled up over something petty, and they'd get too loud or messy to let stay around, so Parker was happy to have a guy of my size around. If anything, my muscles would be getting tense from not getting used enough if I didn't work out at home.

Speaking of tense muscles, as much as I could laugh at the idea of having a guy like Bill as my wingman, Wyatt's comment did remind me how long it had been since I'd bothered trying to find some company for the night. Parker had offered me a few drinks on the house if I ever wanted to chat up someone local, but even if there were anyone in Winchester I was interested in, I liked to keep to myself on my days off.

That's how it had been ever since I moved back into town from Atlanta, and I had been just fine with that.

Back inside The Chisel, the cool air, the smell of bar food, and the sights of frosty beer glasses and cheerful faces welcomed me. Parker gave me a knowing smile from behind the bar, and I gave him a quick nod to let him know the Bill situation was taken care of. I took up my post near the door, leaned back, crossed my arms, and cast a glance around the place.

All was well, especially since most of the crowd at this time of night was made of regulars. Tourists tended to do a double take at the sight of me whenever they blew through The Chisel. Some of the looks from the women told me I wouldn't have too much trouble if I wanted to put myself back on the market, so to speak, but my size and my time in Atlanta had already given me something of a reputation in Winchester—people in small towns thought of the big city as a different world in some ways, and some of that was always going to follow me. I didn't see any need to go adding "playboy" to that reputation.

"There's no chance it isn't him. There's nobody else from around here who'd need a bodyguard," came a voice from the table closest to my left.

I glanced over to see a small group of people in their early twenties huddled around the phone of Dean, the one who'd spoken. He was a woodworking artist in town, and he was sitting in a mixed group of people about his age he always seemed to be with. The group came in for a late drink every now and then, and from pieces of conversation over the past month or so, I'd gathered that Dean was looking for a job. His friends seemed to enjoy checking out the new local job postings with him to make the hunt a little easier, and that was all I could assume I was overhearing.

"That's a hell of a thing for someone from here to be able to put on a resume, huh?" Dean said with a grin on his face. "Bodyguard for the real-ass Jesse Blackwood. No big deal, right?"

"Totally," the woman next to him said. "Does anyone even know what he's doing here? Why is, like, *nobody* talking about it?"

"They're talking about it," said another woman, stirring her drink with the straw. "They're just keeping quiet about it. I feel like the town is kind of… collectively agreeing to be chill about him, y'know?"

"Yeah," Dean agreed. "That's the best you can do. You don't want to chase people like that out of here with too much attention. If I were as famous as him, I don't think I'd leave the house."

That much is true, I thought to myself as they talked.

I recognized the name Jesse Blackwood. My mom had recognized the guy I helped out at brunch this morning about halfway through our meal, and she'd barely been able to contain herself.

Like many of the people in town, my mom was a big fan of *Bannister Heights*, the show this Jesse guy was apparently the star of. I hadn't known that when I'd told the photographer to beat it, but it hadn't made a difference to me. On the drive home, my mom had explained that his character was some bad boy heartbreaker with a romantic soul and a rebellious streak, apparently wrapped up in a lot of very complicated plot lines. And I had to admit he looked the part. Maybe that was just the standard for professional actors who put a lot of effort into their appearances, but when I had seen his face, it had struck me as one that definitely didn't have trouble making hearts beat faster.

"But check out that salary. I could afford a place in LA with that kind of money," Dean added, shaking his head and chuckling. "There's no way it's not him."

"Wouldn't he just hire someone from LA or wherever he's from to bring with him, though?" a guy sitting next to Dean asked.

"Maybe he doesn't want many people knowing he's here," Dean pointed out, waggling his eyebrows.

"Could be. He might be as dramatic as his character," the first woman said, sounding like she was joking.

"That would be… impressive," the second woman said, "but if he's trying to find anyone qualified for this kind of thing, I don't know if he'll find it in Winchester, of all places. I'm pretty sure my parents still don't bother locking the front door."

"Your parents aren't famous," Dean pointed out with a grin, lowering his voice, "and I wouldn't say that so loud, because I can think of at least one guy who fits the bill," he added.

I wasn't facing their table, but I could feel the gazes on my back from their direction. I had figured that would be coming sooner or later, and I held back a smirk. I avoided looking in their direction so they wouldn't know I had been listening in, and when I made eye contact with Parker, who was also looking at his phone, I stood up to head to the end of the bar.

I could keep an eye on the relatively small bar from there, and Parker was always good company.

"Don't tell me you're checking out that job ad too," I said to him with a gruff smile as I leaned against the bar at an angle that would let me keep an eye on the door.

"I am absolutely checking out that job ad too," Parker said, grinning. "They're not wrong, you know."

"What, that it's for the actor guy?" I asked as Jesse's face from this morning materialized perfectly in my memory. "Sure, that tracks."

"Well, that too," Parker said, "but I meant the part about it sounding like a damn good fit for you."

That took me by surprise, and I gave a half chuckle. "Trying to get rid of me already, boss?"

Parker had known me long enough that he knew when I was joking, and we had always had an easygoing relationship. He laughed, then set his phone down with the screen turned toward me to see. I only glanced at it for a moment, but I happened to notice the salary and had to make sure I had read it right.

"Damn," I admitted.

"Right?" said Parker. "All I'm saying is what I've been saying from the start: I love having you here, but you could do a hell of a lot better."

"Uh-huh," I grunted, brushing off the compliment.

Parker meant it in the best possible way. When I first came in to apply for the Help Wanted sign outside The Chisel a couple of years ago, I lied on my resume to downplay my qualifications. The simple fact was that a guy applying at a small-town bar with almost a decade of professional security experience like I had looked odd. I had my reasons, and they were good ones, but once Parker found out how much I really had under my belt, he couldn't understand why I kept showing back up for work.

But he also knew I didn't like talking about it, so most of the time, he didn't bring it up. I appreciated that about him.

"I wouldn't want anyone else to have to haul Bill to the cab," I said, hoping to distract Parker from the subject at hand.

"On the contrary," Parker said with that cunning smile of his, "that nephew I told you about is still looking for a job. I was planning to just hire him to keep the taps clean until he moves, but I could just as easily put him to real work. He's no Marshall, but he's pretty tough, so I could stick him in front of the door to try and fill your shoes."

"Assuming I want to babysit an actor," I pointed out.

"Sure," Parker said, shrugging. "All I'm saying is that money's pretty good, and we both know you'd be a good fit. My nephew's getting hired regardless, so if you wanted to see if it's worth your time, your job here wouldn't go anywhere while you're gone."

"'I appreciate it, boss," I said with a half grin, trying to ignore the interest I felt growing in the back of my mind. "But you don't have to go out of your way for me."

"It's no bother," Parker said. "I know you've been back in town a while now, but it's hard to slow down and adjust to small-town life again after living in the city like you did for so long. This kind of thing might be more like what you're used to, bring a little city life to our quiet neck of the woods."

Privately, I couldn't deny that he was right, and that was about half of the reason I did feel a persistent impulse to check out the job ad when I got home tonight. I loved Winchester, but it was a far cry from the high-paced lifestyle in Atlanta. I hadn't been protecting celebrities, but Parker had good intentions, and hell, Dean had been right: it *would* be a great thing to put on my resume, in case I wanted to leave Winchester again.

And as often as that crossed my mind, whether or not I actually wanted to leave was one of those vexed questions that didn't have a simple answer. It sure didn't have an answer I felt like talking to anyone about, that was for sure.

I opened my mouth to reply, but at that moment, I realized how quiet this area of the bar had gotten. I glanced at the table where Dean and his group sat, and I saw that all of them were not-so-subtly trying to listen to what Parker and I were talking about, and all other conversation at the table had ceased.

Realizing they had been caught, they tried to turn their attention back to their drinks, but Parker had already snorted a laugh at them. I couldn't fault them for eavesdropping, so I just raised an eyebrow at them while Dean gave us a sheepish grin.

"I mean, he's not wrong," Dean said to me.

"*I'd* pay for a bodyguard like you if I needed one," one of the women admitted while giving me a once-over.

"Look, see?" Parker teased. "Now you've gotta go for it, or they'll never leave me alone."

"Doesn't get much more badass than a bodyguard for a star," one of the guys pointed out.

"I could totally see you two looking good together," the other woman added, and to my surprise, something in my gut agreed with her in a way that felt confusing to me, but I didn't pay it much mind.

Before long, there was practically a firing squad of encouragement coming from the table, and I had to run a hand through my hair, chuckling despite myself.

"Well…" I started, and I could have sworn Dean's table leaned in ever so slightly in anticipation. "Sure, I guess it wouldn't hurt to apply," I finally conceded, but the table cheered only half-jokingly, and I shook my head, laughing at them.

There was one other reason I agreed, if I was being totally honest. I wasn't stupid. I knew the photographer who'd harassed Jesse Blackwood this morning had been a paparazzo. Those photographers were notorious for invading people's privacy, and if there was one thing this Jesse guy was probably looking for in a place like Winchester, it was privacy.

I had been through the whole song and dance of settling down in a small town like Winchester as a relative stranger. Hell, I didn't think Dean and Parker would have been so eager to suggest the job to me if it weren't for the fact that they still saw me as somewhat of an outsider, I figured. A decade in "the big city" set me apart from everyone who'd lived here their whole lives, for better or for worse. This guy's situation might not have been exactly the same, but it was close enough that I felt for him.

So if a little personal security could make someone feel welcome here, then that's what I would give him.

JESSE

"So," I began, leaning back in my Adirondack chair on the back deck of my rented lake house, "tell me a little bit about yourself."

The man seated across from me, his elbows braced on his wide-apart knees as he sat perched on the edge of a lounge chair, gave me an arrogant smirk. I already had a bad feeling about this guy, but I was desperate enough to give him a chance to prove me wrong. Maybe he would be less of a jerk than he appeared to be. Then again, maybe I *needed* a jerk. After all, I was working my way through a series of interviews with prospective candidates for the role of personal body-guard while I was staying here in Winchester. My run-in with the sneaky paparazzo at Beulah's Biscuits was a close enough call for my tastes. I had come all the way out here to find some peace and privacy. If I wanted my picture taken by a complete stranger looking to capi-talize on my fame, I would have stayed in Los Angeles.

But of course, if I wanted a bona fide security detail to keep watch and shield me from any potential bottom-feeders, I had to go through the interviewing process first. I was much more accustomed to being on the other side of the table, going to casting calls and auditions all the time back home where I was meant to be judged and measured and compared to every other starry-eyed dreamer who came walking through those doors. Generally, I didn't mind being in that position. Overall, I was pretty confident about my appearance, my charming, affable personality that helped me get along well with any costar or crew member from the lowest crafts services temp to the executive producer and director themselves. I was good at my job, so I felt pretty good going into audition rooms. But being on this side of it was odd. Back home, I had never had to go through a lot of interviews from this angle. Normally, if I wanted to hire someone, I would simply put my wishes out into the world and a friend of a friend would know the perfect person for the position. Easy as pie.

This was different, though. I didn't have a lot of friends or an agent at the ready to help me decide. It was all on me to make the right decision. I was pretty bound and determined to hire locally, in part because I wanted to contribute to the economy and workforce in Winchester while I stayed here. But I also knew that if I were to go through a real security agency, the tabloids who haunt organizations like that, waiting for a little morsel of gossip to blast across the front page of their mad rag, would possibly catch on. The last thing I needed right now was for anyone to raise a stink about my being here. I wanted to blend in as much as possible, and so I had chosen to select my security detail from the pool of... somewhat feasible candidates in town.

Right now, the guy sitting in front of me looked like his photo ought to be splashed underneath the definition for "arrogant" in the dictionary. He also seemed to be roughly as intelligent as a box of gravel.

"Well, I've been a longtime resident of Winchester. Been here ever since I was born," the guy explained, leaning back in his chair and nearly falling out of it. I did my very best to keep the amusement off my face, but this guy was so far up his own bum I doubted he would have noticed it anyway.

"Really? How do you like it here?" I asked, trying to be conversational.

"It's all right. Boring as hell, of course, but there are some pretty hot chicks in town. You know what they say about trailer park girls," he guffawed, giving me an over-the-top wink.

I shuddered. "I'm afraid I don't know what you're talking about," I admitted.

He squinted at me, as though he was realizing for the first time how vastly opposite we were in every way. I wondered if he had even caught on to the fact that I was gay. Or even that I was famous. And then he said something that made it very clear he did not.

"Don't tell my wife, of course, but yeah. If you ever get that itch, ya know, that itch that can only be cured by a hot, young thang—you just let me know. I can tell you exactly where to find them," he blathered on.

By now, I was actually feeling a little sick to my stomach. This guy was beyond cringe-worthy. But I had already blown through several other candidates so far today with no luck, and this douchebag was one of the last. I was starting to get a little defeated, a little desperate. Who the hell in this town could fill the position I needed them to?

"I'm not interested in, uh, hot young women," I said stiffly. "So, you say you have a wife. That's nice. What about a family?"

He wrinkled his nose with disgust. "Babies? Hell no. I tell my wife, 'you look good now, but I don't want you gettin' all bloated and emotional like pregnant ladies do'. I'm not much of a family man. I'm more like a lone wolf," he explained, smirking. I could tell he was, for some reason far beyond my own comprehension, seemingly proud of how much of a raging, useless jackass he was.

"Lovely," I replied flatly. "Well, I think we're just about finished here."

"Damn, man, you move quick! But when you know, you know, you know?" he said inscrutably. I stared at him for a few moments, just taking in how crappy this guy was.

He reminded me of a one-off character we had on Bannister Heights several months ago. A villain, actually. Complete with finger-steepling and mustache-twirling. This guy looked more like a redneck than a criminal mastermind, though. I doubted he had enough brain cells to rub together to be truly dangerous. And then, when he spat a mouthful of chewing tobacco into the grass near our chairs, my decision was firmly cemented. This guy had to go.

"Well. It was nice to make your acquaintance," I said quickly.

"Good to meet you too, man!" he said enthusiastically. He offered his hand for me to shake, but after watching him spit into my yard, I was not at all willing to touch him. So I simply nodded and smiled, giving him a little wave.

"Call me when you need your backup," he said, putting his hands on his knees and pushing himself up to his feet. "I'll come a-runnin'."

"Mhm. Thanks," I said hastily.

Still looking proud of himself, the man plodded off back to his enormous, noisy truck with the gigantic tires. He puttered down the road, the engine coughing and spluttering as he disappeared around the corner and through the narrow, winding road that led through the woods surrounding my rented lake house property on Lake Wren. As soon as the guy was gone, I groaned and buried my face in my hands. What the hell was I supposed to do now? I had already interviewed close to ten potential bodyguards today from the local workforce, and not one of them had perfectly fit the bill. Some of them were very nice and very sincere, but totally unqualified. I was learning that security meant something vastly different out here in the country than it did back in Los Angeles. Here, people seemed awfully eager to suggest carrying a rifle or something. One of the applicants today actually recommended that we set up a series of bear traps in the woods around the lake house. Another told me to build a moat. I had burst out laughing at first, assuming he was joking, but... the deadly serious look on his face sobered me up pretty swiftly.

I was learning quickly that charming, quiet rural life was a double-edged sword. On the one hand, it was absolutely beautiful here. Green, lush forests, quaint little buildings that had been around since the early twentieth century, rolling hills, so many species of flora and fauna that it boggled my brain, and of course—the lake house itself. This place was magical. As I gazed out across the glimmering, dark lake under the midafternoon sunshine, I took a deep breath. At least while I was here at the house, I felt relatively secure. It was far off the beaten path, even for a town like Winchester filled with dirt roads and forest trails. Getting to the house was a bit of a drive from the center of town, which was a relief. I had come here to relax and reboot, and I knew I wouldn't be able to do that if I continued to be surrounded by chattering people like I was in L.A. I needed my alone time, but I also needed someone to defend my alone time and keep it that way. And judging from the pool of not-so-promising candidates I had met today, things were not looking particularly optimistic in that regard.

I sighed, considering again the possibility of reaching out to my contacts back in Hollywood, arranging for one of the big security companies to send me a detail. But that was not only time-consuming and a hassle, it could also be pretty pricey getting someone to fly out here to Winchester for a job. Not many Los Angeles bodyguards were especially eager to leave town and risk missing out on their dream. Most security guys back home, in my experience anyway, were usually doing security as a day job while they toiled away at the Hollywood machine, going to countless auditions when their schedules allowed. To ask one of them to give up the access to L.A. casting opportunities was a big deal. I didn't want to take that away from anyone. And if I did, I'd have to pay them big bucks to assuage my conscience about it. Plus, the fact remained that gossip spread like wildfire through Hollywood. If one person found out that I was hiding out here in Winchester, that bit of news would go viral within hours, and then my quiet, peaceful alone time here would be ruined. I had been stalked by one annoying paparazzo. I certainly didn't want to attract any more of them. Not just for my sake, but also for the sake of the town. The people of Winchester were not seeking fame or notoriety. They just wanted what I wanted: some damn peace and quiet. I was a guest here. The last thing I wanted was to be the reason their lives got flipped upside down. I didn't want my reputation to bleed into the town's history. They were perfectly happy and functional as they were now. Any attention my fame could bring them would disrupt the pace of life here, and I wanted to leave this place exactly as sweet and quaint as I found it. Even if that meant putting my own safety and privacy at risk.

Or just, you know, never leaving the confines of the lake house.

Just when I was starting to give up, ready to turn in and watch some TV on the sofa to try and forget about how unsuccessful the interviewing process had been, I heard the telltale rumble of a vehicle's engine. I stood up and squinted, trying to figure out who the hell was coming this way. The house was pretty well hidden, tucked away on a quiet shore of Lake Wren. It was nearly impossible to accidentally end up here. You really had to know where you were going. Or in my case, just have an extremely reliable GPS in your rental car.

Out of the quiet woods came a truck, but a different one from the guy who had just been here earlier. I didn't recognize this vehicle at first until it dawned on me that I had actually passed a truck similar to it the other day when I'd eaten brunch at Beulah's. I tried to remind myself that there were a hell of a lot of trucks in Winchester and there was no telling whether this was the same one or not. But as it drew closer, it looked more and more familiar. And when I saw the face of the man gripping the steering wheel, my heart nearly thumped out of my chest.

It was, in fact, the big, burly guy who saved me from the paparazzo at Beulah's.

How in the world had he known to come here?

Then I looked down at the sheet of people who had made appointments for interviews with me today, and I realized there was actually a final name on the list I had considered a no-show until now: Marshall Hawkins.

My heart hammered away like crazy in my chest as Marshall pulled up to the house and neatly parked. He paused for a moment. Then I watched as he walked toward me, almost in slow-motion in my mind. He looked every bit as gorgeous and powerful as he had at brunch. He was impossibly handsome, tall and fit in every way. I had to force myself not to openly gawk at him. I had to be professional somehow. I was an actor, after all. I just had to play the role.

I reached out a hand to shake his, and he accepted it gladly. From the moment his palm touched mine, an electric jolt of pure attraction shivered down my spine, rooting me to the spot as I stared into his face. For once, I was literally stunned into silence.

"We met the other day," he said gruffly. "My name's Marshall Hawkins."

"I'm Jesse Blackwell," I murmured back. "Good to see you again."

"You, too," he said courteously. "Should we get started?"

"Oh! Yes. Of course," I said sheepishly, realizing I had been holding his hand a little bit too long now. I hastily withdrew my hand and gestured for him to sit down across from me on the deck. He sat down with a wide stance, and his eyes were locked with mine. This was a man who did not shy away from direct eye contact. I found him both wildly attractive and mildly intimidating at the same time.

Perfect.

Truth be told, I was ready to hire him on the spot after seeing the way he handled that paparazzo the other day, but I knew I needed to at least go through the motions of a real interview. So I cleared my throat and began.

"Mr. Hawkins, can you tell me a bit about your background?" I asked.

"Well, I was born and raised here in Winchester, but I did head up to Atlanta to run security for a small, private company for about ten years before coming back home," he said.

I tilted my head to one side with interest. "What was it that made you come back?"

He smiled, just a quick flicker of warmth that dissipated as quickly as it appeared, and said, "Probably the same reasons you're here."

I grinned. "It's gorgeous here. And quiet."

He nodded. "No place like it on earth, in my opinion. You know, I've been to Lake Wren a thousand times, but I've never seen this place myself."

I hopped up eagerly. "I'll give you a tour!" I said brightly.

Marshall stood up and followed me as I led him around the property, from the convenient wooden docks at the end of the property where the gently lapping waves of Lake Wren began. The property was vast, with beautiful overgrown flowers and hedges that gave a sort of wild sophistication to the place. There was a sunroom with glossy windows and a glass ceiling as well so that you could gaze up at the sky during any kind of weather. The house itself was two stories plus an attic and a basement, with four bedrooms and three bathrooms. It had a massive chef's kitchen with brand-new stainless-steel appliances and cabinets expertly carved and fitted by local woodworkers. The back garden was a lush, fragrant patch of heavily laden apple trees, hibiscus, jasmine, lavender, and wild strawberries. The master bedroom was not only huge but designed with a kitschy minimalism that made me feel instantly at ease. It had a walk-out balcony that overlooked the back yard of the property as well as the lake itself. I showed Marshall every room, spending more time in the guest bedroom closest to the master, both of which had their own en suite bathrooms.

"I'm just in love with the design of this place. A space this size would be astronomically expensive back in Los Angeles," I gushed.

Throughout the tour, I raved and ranted about how much I loved the lake house while Marshall responded with stony-faced nods, mumbles, and grunts. Still, even though he was reticent, I got an overall good feeling about him. Like he was the kind of guy who truly listened to every word out of my mouth, whether it was pertinent or not. I could tell instantly how perceptive and observant he was—both excellent traits in a security detail. By the end of the tour, I was more than ready to hire him, but I had a couple more questions.

"Okay, I'll admit, I'm already prepared to hire you just based on the way you responded to that paparazzo at the diner the other day. You really impressed me with your handling of the situation. But just as a formality, I was wondering if you might have a reference I could call regarding your work history?" I said, smiling.

Immediately, I could sense a change in his mood. He shifted his weight between his feet uncomfortably, looking unwilling to answer my simple question. I was beginning to worry when he managed to heave a sigh and respond.

"I have to admit the place I used to work for shut down a while back. That company no longer exists. However, I can offer you my pay stubs and other documents to show a paper trail if that would help," he offered gruffly.

"That's good enough for me!" I exclaimed. "In fact, I'm hoping to get you started on the payroll as soon as possible. Would you be open to meeting up with me for dinner tonight?"

MARSHALL

LATER THAT DAY, I WAS DRIVING THROUGH THE TWISTING, WOODED roads around Lake Wren, getting closer to Jesse's lake house for the second time that day. I was taking a different route than I usually did, one that was a little more winding and out of the way. Usually, service vehicles were the most traffic these roads got, and it would have been easy for a tourist to get turned around out here. That was exactly why I was taking it. I knew most of the roads around the lake and in town, but if I was going to be this man's bodyguard, I wanted to know the best ways to and from his house.

I wasn't sure what was making me more reluctant about dinner tonight: the fact that it wasn't exactly the most orthodox way to hold a work meeting, or the fact that I had to admit I *really* liked the lake house and was looking forward to spending some time there. The live-in part of this gig was going to take some getting used to, but I sometimes felt like I'd slept away from home in Atlanta as much as I'd actually crashed there, so I was no homebody.

In either case, it had given me an excuse to drive home, throw a few sets of clothes into my bag, and drive back to get changed in time for dinner tonight. Jesse had told me he'd touch base with his agent while I was gone to get all the paperwork involved with hiring me taken care of, or at least started.

Fortunately, I always packed light, and I only had a few outfits I'd need while living with Jesse, so it didn't take me long to head home, pack up, give my mom a quick call to let her know the job had worked out, then head back to the lake house.

I had to admit, a nice dinner somewhere wasn't the kind of thing I usually did, but Jesse wasn't the kind of actor I had been expecting. I was surprised to even have talked to the guy himself. I figured I'd be going through an agent the entire time and that he'd have a team of attendants waiting on him on hand and foot at the house. But so far, he seemed to be more or less what he presented himself to be: an ordinary guy. He was a chatty guy, sure, but that wasn't always a bad thing, so long as he didn't mind me keeping my peace.

I saw Jesse's face in the window of the lake house as I pulled up to it, and he opened the door to meet me as I climbed out of my truck with a couple of bags over my shoulder.

"That was fast!" he said, coming down to the driveway as I approached. "Need a hand with anything?"

"I'm good, thanks," I said, nodding back at the bags. "But I got clothes for tonight and the rest of the job. Just need to get changed."

Jesse was smiling, but he blinked in confusion a couple of times and looked at my bags, then glanced at the empty seats in the front and back of the truck.

"Oh, you mean that's it for clothes?" he asked as I stepped into the house, and he followed close behind.

"Yep," I grunted.

"Wow, you're doing better than me," he said with a laugh. "I'm probably the worst on the planet about packing light. Even before I started acting, the idea of traveling around without at least one suitcase never crossed my mind. I *know* I could just throw a few outfits into a bag and call it done, but then I just think, 'oh, what if I need this or that,' and before I know it, I've already paid for an extra checked bag at the airport."

"Yeah?" was my only response to his ramble, cracking a half-smile down at him as he followed behind me.

"Absolutely, I envy you," he said. "Maybe that'll be something else I can practice while I'm living down here. Honestly, I'm just excited to see more of the town. Even at crowded restaurants, this place feels small, and I can't tell you how nice that is for a change."

"I hear that," I agreed as we headed upstairs to the guest room I was going to be staying in while I'm here.

I stepped inside and surveyed the room once again, even though Jesse already showed it to me earlier, and I took in the decor with a thoughtful stare. It wasn't what I would design, but then again, there was probably a reason I wasn't an interior designer for lake houses. I liked it, though, and that was more than I could say for a lot of places I'd stayed.

"For dinner, I was thinking of this place called The Piedmont Diner. It isn't exactly white tablecloth, but it seems... nice?" he asked, clearly meaning it as a question.

"It's good," I said with a nod, but then I paused. "Not the most 'local' fare, just to warn you. It was started a few years ago by some young folks who wanted food that's more 'organic' if you know what I mean."

Jesse looked mildly surprised, and he appeared to think about that for a moment, then said, "That sounds perfect, actually."

"Health nut, huh?" I suggested as I took out the button-down I had picked out for tonight.

"Me? Really?" Jesse asked, laughing, looking down at himself briefly. "That's flattering, but I don't think anyone would look at me and think 'health nut'. Funny you should mention that, actually, but I'll save that for dinner."

I furrowed my brow, giving him a more proper once-over, and I figured he must have been seeing something I wasn't.

"You look pretty good to me," I said, taking a few steps toward him with my new shirt in hand. "So you must be doing something right."

I saw a little pink appear in Jesse's cheeks, and he neither replied nor moved as I put a hand on the doorframe and peered down at him expectantly. He looked up at me with a mixture of curiosity and what looked like wonder, but when I didn't say anything, he blinked, and I flicked my gaze out the door.

"I uh, need to get changed," I pointed out, which was why I was standing in the doorway in the first place.

"Oh! Right, right, of course," Jesse said, laughing with a charming smile I figured the cameras must have loved, cheeks turning pinker by the second. "I'll give you some privacy and meet you in the living room whenever you're ready."

He slipped out of the bedroom, and after I closed my door, I had to chuckle. The guy was a character on screen and off it seemed.

A few minutes later, I came down the stairs to the living room, where Jesse was already sitting on the couch with an e-reader in his hands. He glanced up at me when I reached the bottom of the stairs, then did a double take with wider eyes that made me look down at myself, thinking I'd forgotten to button something.

But no, everything was in place the way I'd put it on. I wore a simple dark gray button-down, with sleeves rolled up to my forearms, slim but comfortable black pants, and the same kind of black shoes I'd worn when I'd been running security in Atlanta: professional yet comfortable and easy to move fast in, if need be.

"Something wrong?" I asked, glancing back up at him.

"No, not at all," he said, standing up and setting the e-reader down. "You just clean up well. I forgot where I was for a second."

"Thanks," I grunt. "Probably redundant to say you do too, right?"

Jesse looked fantastic, but I had been expecting that. True to what I'd expected, his idea of dressing for a nice-ish dinner out was much nicer than what most people in Winchester would be dressing like. He wore a white short-sleeved Henley that was mostly unbuttoned, paired with black chinos and modest dress shoes. I wasn't up to date on all the latest names in fashion, but it all looked like designer wear, but not the type that screamed "rich and obnoxious."

Hell, if I stayed here long enough, I might need to jot down a few fashion tips from him. He wore it all well, as if it was made just for him—just a little tight around the waist, which I actually thought added a little something to the ensemble.

Why was I putting this much thought into Jesse's outfit? I brushed the thoughts away as Jesse laughed and waved off the comment.

"You don't have to exaggerate. I know I stick out like a sore thumb," he said.

"A sore thumb that knows how to dress," I countered. "Let's get going if you'd like to eat early. I'll drive."

"Why don't we take a cab?" he asked, following me out the door after patting himself down, silently mouthing a quick checklist to make sure he had everything he needed. "I don't want you to feel like my driver or anything fancy like that."

I paused, thinking for a moment, and then I took out my phone. That was a fair point, I supposed, and I was pleasantly surprised that he had been considerate enough to think about that. I texted Wyatt, asking him to meet me here and not say a word about my "friend," and nodded at Jesse.

"Done. I know a good one."

If there was one cab driver I could trust to keep his mouth shut for me, it was Wyatt. Half an hour later, we were getting dropped off, and Wyatt was driving away with a hefty tip.

The Piedmont Diner was an interesting establishment, and it wasn't a diner in the sense the locals were used to. We were in the closest thing Winchester had to a downtown area, which consisted mostly of a few blocks of the oldest buildings in town. The restaurant building used to be an old post office, which was why it was on the corner of an intersection that featured a handful of office buildings and an equally ancient bakery. If it weren't for the lovingly hand-painted sign sticking out and hanging from the door, it would have been easy to miss.

But even though it looked like something I'd have seen in a hipster neighborhood of Atlanta, the small-town effect was impossible to shake. As soon as we stepped through the doors, I saw that the hostess who promptly made her way over to seat us was one of the young women from The Chisel who had been encouraging me to apply for this job in the first place. I kept my face stony, and I internally breathed a sigh of relief when she restrained her obvious excitement and invited us to follow her as if we were nobody special. A minute later, we were seated next to a beautiful painting of the town about midway through the restaurant, which was as bustling as it ever got around here: no wait, but there were still more than enough diners to show that this place drew a crowd.

I found myself grateful for that, too, as well as the fact that the hostess didn't seat us right in front of the street side window. I didn't know why I was worrying this much about Jesse finding Winchester comfortable. It wasn't like he was a helpless brat. But he seemed to love the place, and it had felt good to watch him walk through the place with a charming smile.

He's an actor, I reminded myself. *It's his job to be charismatic. He's just plain good at it.*

"So," Jesse said, steepling his fingers after our waiter served us some waters and took our drink orders—Jesse got wine; I got a beer. "If you're going to be living at the lake house, it might help to explain a few things."

"Let me guess. You're on the run?" I asked, half joking. "That's fine. We'll just add hazard pay to my contract."

"Not quite," Jesse said after covering his mouth to keep from laughing into his water. "But good to know I have someone I can go to if I ever need to rob a bank," he joked back, and I tipped my head with a shadow of a smile.

"Southern hospitality," I said.

"We joke, but I guess 'on the run' isn't too far off," he said on a more serious note. "At least, that's what it felt like at first. I…" He paused, struggling with the right words for a moment. "You don't watch variety type shows around primetime, by chance, do you?"

"No."

"Well, don't take this as a suggestion to start," he said with a chuckle. "I probably shouldn't start with this story, it's…honestly kind of silly, but I don't want to come off like some rich guy vacationing down here for fun."

"Nothing wrong with fun," I pointed out as our drinks arrived, and I gave a nod to the waiter.

"True," Jesse said. "Maybe that's not the right way to put it. So, a few months ago, I agreed to an interview on a talk show with a well-known comedian. I was expecting to get teased, so this isn't a story about how I got my feelings hurt or anything," he clarified. "I don't know how obvious it is, but I don't have the same... *figure* I was known for on screen in my twenties," he said.

I raised an eyebrow because Jesse's figure looked more than just pretty good to me, but I supposed everyone had their preferences.

"The guy was just breaking the ice, and he introduced me as the star of *Bannister Heights*, quote, 'whose notorious shirt buttons pop off a little too easily these days'."

My second eyebrow went up, and I blinked.

"Sounds like an ass," I said, feeling oddly defensive of Jesse, but I supposed that was a good impulse for my job.

"It was fine, really," Jesse said, and I could tell by his tone that he really meant it. "But it kind of stuck with me whether I wanted it to or not, and it got me thinking. I'm not originally from L.A., you know?"

I shook my head.

"I'm from a small town outside Knoxville, Tennessee. I know, I don't sound like it anymore, but I was born and raised around there. Didn't move out of state until I went to college. It... took a while to get used to living in the city."

That took me by surprise. Jesse had so far seemed all right by city standards, but I hadn't pegged him as being that close to home.

"How so?" I asked, curious.

"It's kind of a paradox," he said, glancing toward the window at the front of the restaurant before looking back at me. "People seem to care about you less, but they're more blunt...sometimes in a good way," he added, smiling, "and you forget what it's like not to have everything so easy to get. Life's faster and bigger, but kind of smaller, too. It's hard to explain."

"No, I actually know the feeling," I said, as surprised as Jesse to hear myself say it. "Adjusting to Atlanta was like that."

"That's right. I remember that, I was hoping you'd felt kind of the same thing," he said, leaning forward. "Did you know anyone when you moved there?"

I thought about my uncle for a moment, then shook my head. I thought I knew him pretty well when I first went over there to work for him. I had been wrong.

"No."

"Me either, and god, isn't it daunting?" he said, seeming like he was excited to get all this out. "You grow up thinking people are exaggerating when they say it feels like a city can eat you alive, but…"

"They couldn't be more right," I admitted, thinking back to my first week in Atlanta. "People talk differently. All business, less small talk. Fast-paced way of living. Some people prefer one or the other, but it was the adjustment that took me by surprise," I explained.

"Exactly!" Jesse said, beaming. "You start to miss the empty roads, the sounds of the woods…"

"The quiet," I said, nodding solemnly. "Didn't sleep a wink my first week there."

"You should have seen the look on my agent's face when I asked him for honest-to-god earplugs," Jesse said, and I couldn't hold back a smile at the thought. "It was the only way I could deal with the sounds of traffic in the background. And to think locals can't sleep *without* it."

"I should've thought of earplugs," I grumbled.

"But anyway, you get what I'm talking about when I say the comment was kind of a wakeup call that I'd sort of lost myself a little, right?" he asked, settling into a more serious tone again.

"I do now," I said, surprised by just how true it was.

I hadn't spoken to many people about it since coming back to Winchester, but Jesse had pretty succinctly described how it felt to move from a cozy small town like Winchester to a bustling city like Atlanta. It wasn't nearly as big as L.A., but the culture shock had still been intense. And that was still in the southeast. I couldn't imagine what a shock it would be to come from a place like this to L.A. Jesse must have been one hell of an adaptable guy.

35

This pampered actor was turning out to be more interesting than I'd expected.

"Well, we're between filming seasons on the show," Jesse went on. "And it got me thinking. Maybe it would be good to take some time to reconnect to my roots, as embarrassing as that sounds," he added, blushing.

I shook my head, dismissing his idea. I had found myself pining after the familiar sights and sounds of home before too long when I moved away. There was no shame in that.

"And maybe lose a few pounds while I'm at it," he added, looking down at himself. "I don't really want to treat this like a vacation. It is in some ways, but I want to feel some of the things I haven't felt since I moved away, you know? The smell of country air, feeling and looking healthy, drives on country roads under starry nights."

"I hear you," I said, nodding.

It sounded like Jesse was here doing what I wanted to find here. He was soul-searching, clearly, and it just happened to have a physical side to it.

"I love acting, don't get me wrong," he said. "And in a month or so when I need to get back out west to start filming again, I'll be happy to, but in the meantime, I want to find a way to feel less...I'm not sure what the word I'm looking for is."

"Unmoored," I said, and Jesse snapped his fingers.

"Yeah, that's exactly it," he said, his surprise melting away to an impressed look. "Well, that and trimming down a little, but I don't know if I could put that in quite as few words. Speaking of trimming down, I guess we should get around to looking at the menu."

We perused the options and ordered, but the food turned out to be the least interesting part of the dinner. After breaking the ice and downing our drinks before the food even arrived, I found it a lot easier to talk to Jesse about some of the odds and ends of getting settled after moving. Jesse's hometown even sounded more like Winchester than I'd expected.

"Why Winchester, though?" I finally asked as we were finishing our food.

"What, as in, why did I choose it?" he asked. "That's actually total coincidence. My parents took me on a couple of road trips as a kid, and we stopped in Winchester along the way. My dad still has this really nice set of woodworking tools he couldn't resist buying, but he never touched them," he said, chuckling.

"Mm. People here are spoiled for wood," I said, patting the locally made wooden chairs we were sitting in. "Never met someone from anywhere else who really knows how to handle it like we do."

"I bet," Jesse said with a laugh.

I raised an eyebrow at him curiously, and that seemed to take him off guard. He blushed and scratched the back of his head, and if I didn't know better, I'd think he looked almost flustered.

"Everything okay?" I asked.

"Great! This food is amazing," he added. "And *probably* not as much of an artery-killer as that breakfast place, but that's a problem for future-Jesse to worry about. Should we call the cab soon?"

I nodded and took out my phone to do just that as the waiter came to collect our plates and leave our check, but even as I texted Wyatt, I couldn't help but shake the feeling I finally recognized, and I wasn't entirely sure how to process this information.

I didn't want dinner with Jesse to end.

JESSE

As I stood outside in the balmy night air, I couldn't help but feel tingles of adrenaline and attraction running frantically through my veins. My stomach was churning, and it had absolutely nothing to do with the delicious food we had just enjoyed inside the restaurant. My stomach was reacting just as my heart was. Just as my mind was. Everything running in wild, incoherent circles, spurred on by the feelings of intense admiration welling up inside me. It was like every moment I spent with Marshall, the better I understood him, and yet he always left me longing for more. More eye contact. More truth-spilling. More soft, gruff confessions under the moody lights of the restaurant. I wanted to know everything about this man. I was fascinated by him, by every move he made and every word he said. I could tell he wasn't quiet because he was unintelligent or uninteresting.

In fact, I found it to be just the opposite. He was the most intriguing man I had ever met, which was saying something. After all, I had been living in the town of crazy personalities and star-studded events for a long time now, so I would have liked to think I had a pretty high standard for what I found curious or enchanting. I met interesting people all the time back home. Everybody had their specific quirks, their neatly carved niche into which they could fit and use as a means of marketing themselves to casting directors and artists all over Los Angeles. People back home were constantly doing eccentric activities, changing up the way they dressed, the way they spoke, how they carried themselves, even what kind of car they drove. People worked their asses off to curate precisely the kind of "weird" they thought would best help them stand out and make a lasting impression. We were all competing to see who could be the most outlandish, the most memorable at the end of the day.

But Marshall was different. He was genuine. He was authentic. He was interesting to me without having to resort to the usual gimmicks and tricks people in L.A. relied upon to stake their specific pop cultural claims. In fact, everything about Marshall seemed purposely guided toward keeping an air of thick mystique around himself. He was plain and open in the way he talked about things, no guile to speak of. And yet, he still found a way to keep things hidden. To hold back just enough to keep me guessing and longing for more.

I craved understanding. I wanted to know what he dreamed of at night, what his favorite food was, what his usual drink order at a bar was. I wanted to know about his family, his friends, his lifestyle. I wanted to know what made him tick, what got him out of bed in the morning. In Los Angeles, everyone seems to be an extrovert, always looking for the next opportunity to overshare and wax poetic about one's own struggles and accomplishments. Marshall, on the other hand, seemed perfectly patient and content to hold things back and let the truths trickle out slowly over time. He was a quiet man, but he was no shrinking violet, either. He was traditional in a lot of ways, but I could sense that there was something off-kilter about him in a way that gave me an itch I just couldn't scratch. He made me want to gaze into his eyes and listen to him say anything, absolutely anything, as long as he said it to me.

I kept trying to remind myself not to get too wrapped up in obsessing over my brand-new security detail. After all, no matter how utterly fascinating I found him, at the end of the day, he was just here to do his job. He was here to protect me, to stand back and keep guard over my privacy. Back in Los Angeles, I would have barely interacted with the security team my agent would hire for me. That was the way it worked. I was the actor, the object in need of defense, and they were the doers and the preventers. And never the twain should meet. That was the rule. Maybe it was a little anti-quated. In the past, I had certainly felt a little odd sometimes refer-ring to my hired help as... well, hired help. Even though I was absolutely, unapologetically a cog in the Hollywood machine, I still preferred to think of myself as a genuine person, not just some cari-cature of a soap opera actor. I could certainly ham it up on-screen. That was my job. But off-camera, I was a huge admirer of authentic-ity. I liked to see real people living their real lives. I liked to talk to people who were down to earth, who knew themselves on a deep, natural level. In a town packed full of phonies and fakes, one honest conversation was like finding a needle in a haystack. Hell, even some of my most beloved friends and costars could be a tad bit shallow at times. But not Marshall. He was real. One hundred percent real. Through and through. And that drew me to him like a moth to a flame.

"So, the cab driver... you know him?" I said, making small talk as we waited quietly for the taxi to arrive and pick us up.

Marshall nodded. "Yes. He and I go way back. As you can probably imagine, there aren't exactly a ton of taxi drivers here in town. Most folks have their own wheels. But it works for Wyatt. He's reliable and honest, not to mention probably the safest driver in the state," he said.

"Wow. I feel honored to have ridden in his taxi, then," I said, smiling.

A flicker of warmth crossed Marshall's impossibly handsome face, giving my heart a little flutter. He nodded slowly.

"He's a good one. Not a total rarity though. You'll find that out soon enough. Most people here in Winchester are genuinely good, honest, hardworking folks. This community can be a little dull, a little quiet, but you won't find a single town in the country filled with better people. Sure, there are a few bad apples, but they don't spoil the bunch," he said.

"I believe it," I replied honestly, gazing at him sidelong. I didn't give breath to the other thing I wanted to say: *I believe it because you're one of the good ones. Maybe the best.*

A moment later, the taxi came slowly rolling up to the curb outside the restaurant. A faint smile hitched itself to Marshall's lips as he greeted Wyatt the cab driver for the second time tonight. The driver gave us a polite nod and unlocked the car. Wanting more privacy, I slid into the backseat, thinking that Marshall would get up front in the passenger's seat. But to my surprise, he slid in beside me. I swallowed hard, my body heating up just from the sheer proximity of this incredibly good-looking bear of a man. I could feel the raw heat and power rolling off his body in waves. I could smell his aftershave, tinged with his own deep, musky, delicious, masculine scent. Everything about him was intoxicating to my senses, and I had to force myself not to let it show. After all, our working relationship had just begun. I needed to maintain my composure.

"Have a nice dinner?" Wyatt asked politely, glancing back at us in the overhead mirror as the taxi pulled away from the curb and out onto the main road through the town of Winchester.

"Yes. It was great," I said, although I had already forgotten what I had even ordered.

Truth be told, I had been so deeply distracted by Marshall that I might as well have eaten a bowl of sawdust and not even noticed. I was sure there had to be some truly tempting items on that menu, but none of them were half as appetizing as my brand new bodyguard.

"A little rich for my tastes, but still good," he said.

"The wife keeps askin' me to take her there on a date night," Wyatt shared with a smile of pure love. "I'm more of a hot wings-and-fries kind of guy, but for my girl? I'll go just about anywhere. We just have to find a Friday night where we're both off work and someone can watch the kids."

"I think one of the girls I've worked with at The Chisel is a former nanny. I can probably get her name and information for you if that would help," Marshall offered kindly.

Wyatt grinned from ear to ear. "Why, that'd be fantastic. Thanks, man."

"Don't mention it," Marshall said softly, looking out the window.

Again, I felt my heart fluttering like the wings of a butterfly. He was just such a good guy. A little brusque, a little aloof, but there was no mistaking the good soul inside of him.

Then, suddenly, as we were turning off the main road and onto a narrow side road that would eventually splinter off into even smaller roads, most of which were unpaved, Marshall sat up straighter. A look of predator-like vigilance appeared on his sharp features, and I immediately worried. He was looking around out the windows, finally turning around to look out the back windshield. His expression turned even darker, and he swore under his breath.

"Shit," he murmured.

"What's up? You forget your wallet at the restaurant or somethin'? I don't mind at all goin' back for it," Wyatt offered.

"No. It's not that." Marshall sighed. "We're being followed."

My stomach dropped, and I began to feel ill.

"Wait. What? Followed? By whom?" I rambled, looking around. Marshall quickly laid a firm hand on my shoulder, intensity flashing in his eyes.

"Don't turn around. Don't make eye contact. Slide down in the seat, keep your head down, Jesse," he ordered. "They want you to turn and look. That's their money shot."

"Shit. You're right," I mumbled, sinking down in the seat and trying to make myself as small and unobtrusive as possible.

"What do you want me to do, boss?" Wyatt asked calmly.

Marshall thought for a moment, then leaned forward so that he could point over Wyatt's shoulder up ahead. "See that third left turn down there? Take that way," he commanded.

"You got it," Wyatt agreed.

"Who's back there?" I asked worriedly.

"Looks like the same guy as before. That asshole from Beulah's," Marshall grunted.

"Oh fuck," I groaned, rolling my eyes. "Can't he give it a rest?"

"Don't worry. We'll shake him. He doesn't look local. And nobody knows these back roads like Wyatt and I do," Marshall assured me.

"You got that right," Wyatt said, giving me a wink in the rearview mirror.

I kept my head down so that the photographer couldn't snap a photo of me as Marshall directed and conspired with Wyatt on where to go. From this far down in the seat and with night falling dark around us, I couldn't see much outside the windows except the dusky tops of trees waving slightly in the soft breeze. However, I could feel it when the car would veer left, then a sharp right, then another right, then a left. I felt it when the tires rolled from relatively smooth asphalt to loose gravel to bumpy, barely maintained dirt roads. For all I knew, we were just driving in big circles. In Los Angeles, this kind of ride would have been truly harrowing, but I instinctively trusted Marshall and Wyatt so much that it was almost fun. By the time we had finally shaken off the confused paparazzo, we were all feeling exhilarated and in high spirits. I even heard Marshall laugh softly as he gave the taxi driver a solid high five.

Then he turned to me, his eyes still bright and glowing with excitement, and said in a surprisingly warm voice, "You're safe now. You can sit up normally."

I wriggled back into a regular sitting position and smiled at him.

"Thank you so much. Wow. You two really saved my ass back there," I gushed.

"No problem," Wyatt remarked. "That was fun as hell."

Marshall chuckled. "That's my job, isn't it?" he said to me.

I nodded, feeling as though my heart might burst out of my chest at any moment.

"Guess that's true," I replied. His eyes stayed locked on mine for a few intense, electric moments, and then his gaze flitted down to briefly linger over my lips. A shock of desire coursed through my body.

Was he feeling what I was feeling?

No. That was impossible... right?

When Wyatt pulled up to the lake house, we hastily gave him a massive tip, and he saluted us, then went off on his way. Marshall and

I looked at each other, standing close together, nearly elbow to elbow as we watched the cab disappear.

"That was close," I said.

"That's why you've got me," he said, in a way that sent a tingle down my spine.

I could see the pure adrenaline pulsing through his body just as it did mine, and we looked at each other for so long it might have been minutes or hours—it didn't matter. Because before either of us could think too much about it, we had stepped closer, completing the gap between us until his hands were on my body and reaching up to cup my face, his fingers tangling in my hair. Restless energy flowed through our fingers as we grappled together, his lips pressed against mine. I was so shocked and amazed that my mind went blank. All that mattered was getting inside the house, getting some privacy, and getting as close to this magnificent, surprising man as I possibly could.

We stumbled up the front steps and staggered into the foyer, still clutching one another as his tongue probed into my mouth and his hands roved down to grab my ass. I groaned against his lips, rocking against him as he pinned me into the wall. He pulled back for just a moment to stare into my eyes, a silent question hovering in the air between us.

Do we?

Should we?

Will we do it anyway?

The answers, clear on his face as well as in my gut were yes, yes, and absolutely. Still, I felt the need to ask aloud. I didn't want there to be any doubt lingering.

As I sank to my knees before him, seeing the flush of wine, adventure, and adrenaline on his gorgeous face, I asked him, "Do you want this? Is this okay?"

He nodded.

"Are you sure?" I asked again.

Marshall unzipped his pants and tugged down his boxers just enough to let his massive, glorious cock spring free. I stared at it wide-eyed, my mouth already watering. I dragged my eyes away to look up into his face again.

"Are you sure-sure?" I asked quietly.

"Yes," he said emphatically, indicating to me that he was far more interested in action than talk. And right now, that was perfectly fine with me.

I leaned forward and gently tugged the head of his cock into my mouth, groaning with appreciation as his thickness stretched my cheeks to accommodate it. I wrapped my arms around his muscular thighs to steady myself as I gradually took him into my mouth, inch by inch until the tip was brushing against the back of my throat. Marshall moaned, rutting gently into my mouth, essentially fucking my face while I held on tight. I slurped down every inch with delight, tasting the salty bead of precome glistening at the tip, letting my tongue flick around the sensitive underside of his cock while Marshall's fingers tangled in my hair.

He guided me with his fingers, pulling me back and pressuring me to push all the way down, taking his full length again and again until I was nearly coughing. My eyes watered, but I was having the time of my damn life. Every little twitch and moan Marshall gave me only spurred me to take more of him into my mouth, to bob up and down faster. I reached up to wrap my hands around his length, pumping in tandem with the pressure of my lips and tongue. Before long, Marshall was groaning and gritting his teeth, his hips pistoning back and forth as he pummeled his cock down my throat. Even though I could tell he was not accustomed to doing this with another man, he seemed totally in control. He used his hands on my head to guide me, to mastermind the whole situation. And I couldn't get enough of it. I had never thought of myself as a particularly submissive guy, but with Marshall it was different. I felt completely safe with him. I trusted him with my whole heart. I knew he would never lead me astray, would never intentionally harm me.

I wanted to make sure he understood just how appreciative I was.

So I pleasured him with gusto, fully enjoying every moment, every growl and groan that rolled out of his throat. Finally, he began to stiffen up, his whole body tensing. His muscles clenched, his breathing quickened, and he grabbed my head in his hands, holding me in place while he shuddered through a tremendous orgasm, his hot spunk rolling down my throat as I swallowed it all eagerly. When he let go, I voraciously lapped up every last drop as he stood there with his eyes shut, still recovering from the powerful aftershocks of intense pleasure.

Finally, I stood up and wiped my mouth. Then, in comfortable, sleepy silence we walked to the master bedroom, falling into bed together. The excitement of the day and evening had gotten to us, and we all but collapsed under the sheets with total exhaustion. I fell asleep with a big smile on my face, the taste of Marshall still clinging to my tongue.

* * *

THE NEXT MORNING, I snapped awake out of a dream, sitting up with wide eyes. I glanced at the clock on the nightstand. It was seven o'clock. Birds were chirping and flitting around outside my bedroom window, the sun shining brightly. All at once, the memories of last night came rushing back to me, and I turned to look at the spot beside me in bed.

My stomach dropped when I realized that it was empty.

Marshall was gone.

MARSHALL

THUNDER RUMBLED IN THE DISTANT STORM CLOUDS AS I STOOD AT THE end of the driveway, at the very edge of the lake house property where the wood line opened up. My arms were crossed, and my feet were planted firmly in the ground as I stared up at an old black gum tree that stood proudly a few feet off the road.

I was scouting out good locations around the property for security cameras. Jesse's lake house was very nice, but it hadn't been built with celebrities in mind. Even well-off vacationers in this part of the state weren't the types who generally wanted or needed security cameras, but it would be worth the investment for Jesse, I thought.

And every time I thought about him, the taste of his lips came back to my mind with a vivid intensity that made my heart skip a beat.

I shook my head, running a hand over my face and taking out my phone to photograph the tree for reference before I marched onward to continue my survey. I had been doing this for about an hour, and I had started more or less as soon as I got up.

Seeing Jesse's sleeping face in the dawn sunlight had made me want to wake him up by scooping him into my arms and hugging him tight to me, letting him feel what he could stir up inside me by pressing my hips against his so that my hardening cock throbbed against his tight ass. I wanted to wrap my hand around that cock and do what we did last night in a whole new light, literally.

For what had to be the tenth time this morning, I tried to clear my head of those thoughts and stay focused on the task at hand. My heavy footsteps carried me around the perimeter of the property that wasn't on the lake's banks, and I snapped pictures of a few more trees and their possible ranges of sight they could detect.

For one particularly advantageous tree that I thought could give me a panoramic view of the whole property's front, I put my hands on a sturdy, low-hanging branch and hoisted myself up. I climbed until I was about eight feet up.

From this high vantage point, I had to admit I had the kind of view that photographers would kill for. I thought about installing some spikes of some kind to discourage trespassers from taking advantage of it, but for the time being, I decided to take a few pictures from up here in case I forgot about this later and needed a reminder to put up at least one camera in this tree.

Through even my phone's humble camera lens, I had a stunning view of the lake house and the glowing lake beyond it. The shimmering waters caught the golden morning light and amplified it many times over, and the calm waters gently lapping at the banks gave me a deep sense of peace that I hadn't realized I'd been craving all morning. I felt a little more centered up there...and after last night, that was something I needed in a big way.

But before I could let myself earnestly think about that, my camera lens caught something that got my attention. I had just snapped a picture of the lake that included the roof of the house, but when I panned the camera lens down to the door of the house, I saw Jesse stepping out of the front door, looking around curiously with two mugs of what I assumed was coffee in his hands.

He didn't see me up here in the tree because not many people ever thought to look up when looking for someone, but I waved to get his attention as soon as I saw him coming out. His eyebrows went up when he saw me, and I saw a laughing but mildly confused smile cross his face as he made his way toward the tree, dressed in a large black robe and moccasins. I was already in jeans and a white tank top to make it easy to move around the property without getting hot and sweaty in the humid morning, but I had to admit, he looked pretty cozy.

"Morning!" he greeted me as I climbed down to a low point in the tree where a thick branch grew out from the trunk, allowing me to wedge myself down and still stay in the tree while Jesse handed me my coffee. "I was worried for a second, didn't realize you had gotten up so quietly."

"I'm not going anywhere," I assured, accepting the coffee and raising the mug to him. "Thanks. Sleep all right?"

"Good, good," he said, nodding and shifting his weight from foot to foot. "What are you, uh… are you getting some morning exercise?"

Admittedly, finding your bodyguard in a tree before eight in the morning might be unusual, but then again, we'd had a very unusual night.

"That's a perk," I admitted. "No, I'm surveying the property. I want to see if your agent will approve some security cameras. I'm not positive that photographer from last night knows where you live, but if it doesn't stay that way, I want to have eyes around the house."

I hopped down from the tree, and I landed with a thump just in front of Jesse. A little coffee spilled out of my mug, but I swiped a few drops from my knuckle as Jesse raised his eyebrows, watching me.

"How would you feel about that?" I asked, snapping him out of it.

"Oh! Sure, sure, no harm in that, if you think it's necessary. You're the expert. So, you've just been doing some work?" he asked, glancing around as if expecting something more.

"Yep," I said simply, making my way toward the small pier behind the house. "I think I might set one up out there at the edge of the pier to look back on the house. That's about as good a vantage point as I can hope for from a flat lake. Hmm…"

Jesse followed close behind me, not saying anything else for a few moments, but before long, he broke the silence.

"This is all great. By the way, you're doing a far better job than I'd expected, in all honesty," Jesse said. "But I have to say, when I first woke up this morning, I wasn't sure if last night was…"

He hesitated for only a moment, probably trying to find the right words before coffee in the morning. I'd have trouble with that too, so I decided to spare him the effort.

"Last night was unprofessional of me," I said, coming to a slow stop and turning to face him when we had reached the beginning of the pier.

Jesse looked surprised by my words, but I went on before he could say anything, looking down at him with a simple, straightforward expression that I hoped still showed some concern. I had been avoiding letting my own mind dwell on last night, but that didn't mean Jesse's thoughts didn't matter. In fact, I thought they mattered more than my own, in this case.

"Let me level with you," I said, rubbing the back of my neck. "I'm not great at talking about this kind of thing. I acted on impulse last night. If I did anything to make you uncomfortable…"

"Me?" Jesse said, wide-eyed, and I was relieved to see a smile spread across his face. "Are you kidding? I was coming out here to ask you the same thing. I'd never want to think I somehow pressured you into anything."

I grinned, Jesse laughed, and we both stood there for a moment over our steaming coffees, tension broken but leaving us both with a touch of embarrassment.

"Not at all," I affirmed, shaking my head and taking a moment to choose my words carefully. "Last night was good. Very good."

"I'm glad," Jesse breathed, cheeks going that familiar shade of pink that seemed inevitable whenever we were around each other. "I could have sworn last night would have been too *new* for you."

"New? Yes," I said, reaching for his chin and holding it for a moment with a gruff smile down at him. "Regrets? None. I like you."

"Your first time with a man?" he said. "You could have fooled me."

"I'm happy with last night if you are," I said, lowering my hand. "But I work through my feelings with my hands. Sorry to worry you this morning. Believe it or not, I stay busy to keep from overthinking things. If I didn't have anything to do, I would have spent all morning wondering if I said something wrong last night."

"Believe me, everything you said last night was just right," Jesse assured me, and I had to laugh at myself for being as proud of that as I was.

Jesse's personality was infectious to me, and I liked knowing that something about me could make him happy. Hindsight was 20/20, and I knew now that was probably why I felt some of the things I felt about Jesse before everything boiled over—in a damn good way.

I had always considered myself a terse speaker. It wasn't because I was trying to be rude, but I just felt that if there was a simple way to say something, then you ought to say that and not beat around the bush. That was who I had always been, and that made it awkward that I now felt the need to say something more to Jesse. The way he was looking at me, I sensed it showed, but he didn't push me either. That part was surprising, but it was a welcome surprise.

"In that case, maybe we'll have to have another 'talk' sometime," Jesse said with a flirty, teasing undertone that warmed my heart.

"Maybe we will," I flirted right back, winking at him as I took a swing of my coffee. "Damn, you make a good pot of coffee. In the meantime, let's see about some security around here. I'm still your bodyguard, after all," I added with a wolfish grin that made Jesse bite his lip before I walked past him toward my truck.

"So you said security cameras would be on the shopping list," he said, following me across the property as we sipped on hot coffee and felt the dewy grass underfoot. "Do you know how to install all that?"

"Not everyone in my line of work does," I admitted as I reached the truck and rummaged through the back seat. "But I took the time to learn because I wasn't sure if I could trust the private companies to handle it themselves. It's not like the people setting these things up want to grift you, but it helped me catch some mistakes in the past."

"Impressive," Jesse admitted.

"All the better to keep an eye on you," I said over my shoulder, and I didn't even have to look at his face to know I'd earned a blush. "But in the meantime," I said, finally uncovering a spool of wire and holding it up. "There are more old-fashioned techniques for security."

It was a trip wire alarm, as I told Jesse as I walked him back out to some of the areas where I wanted to set them up.

"Simplest kind of security system there is," I explained as I sized up the tree trunks I was considering before getting to work. "It's no state-of-the-art camera system, but it'll do in a pinch."

"This won't hurt anyone, will it?" he asked, hovering at a reasonable distance as I worked, but interested in the process. "I want to keep paparazzi away, but I don't want to hurt a hiker or anything. One of the guys I interviewed before you was suggesting bear traps, and I... wasn't totally sure if he was kidding, honestly," he said, chuckling.

"No," I said. "If someone trips this, it'll make a loud bang that might make 'em piss themselves, but it won't hurt. See these little red caps?" I asked, holding one up to Jesse, who nodded. "These come from a toy gun. Mostly harmless, especially the way I'm using them here, but they're loud as hell. I'm attaching them to this mousetrap here. Simplest way I can explain it is that if someone walks over the wire I'm setting up between these trees, it'll trip the mousetrap, and *bang*. Thanks to how well the lake carries sound, we *will* know if someone's here who isn't supposed to be."

Jesse stared as I finished setting up the first, and he shook his head a little.

"Just like that?" he asked.

"Just like that," I said, crossing my arms and nodding at my handiwork. "Now that you mention it, though, a bear trap might not have been such a bad idea."

Jesse nearly spit out the sip of coffee he was taking, and I chuckled.

"Don't worry, I was thinking of fake ones," I said, not mentioning the fact that I totally just wanted to see Jesse's face at that prospect. "What I might do is buy a few, file down the tips, and modify them so they're just useless metal. Then I'll leave them somewhere obvious, probably do a half-assed job of making them seem hidden. That way, anyone who sees them will think we mean business, and anyone brave enough to keep going after that will be looking out for bigger traps, not subtle ones like trip wires."

I dusted off my hands and marched off to the next couple of trees, leaving Jesse staring after me thoughtfully before catching up.

"You really put a lot of thought into this," he remarked. "Let me guess. You've got to have a cabin in the woods that's locked up tighter than Fort Knox, right?"

"I wish," I said. "I rent a place not far from the mechanic. Nothing special, just a small house I keep clean. I don't leave out bear traps, though. Burglary isn't a problem around here, but if there's some brass-balled punk who wants to break into my house and tangle with me that bad, I'd like to meet 'em," I said, enjoying Jesse's silence at that ominous statement, but I didn't let myself smile until I had my back turned to him.

I wasn't kidding about petty crime being a nonissue in Winchester, but I wasn't that eager to tear someone's arms off, either. The simple fact was that I didn't have anything worth stealing besides a TV that would be worthless next year anyway, and I didn't think any locals in their right mind would want to get on my bad side. I wasn't always proud of that fact, but it meant I didn't have to worry about it as much.

Over the next few hours, punctuated by a trip to the hardware store, I set up a DIY security perimeter around the property while Jesse alternated between hovering around me to make conversation or heading back inside for a few minutes. But just like yesterday, I was surprised not to mind his presence in the slightest. In fact, I felt a smile tug at the corners of my mouth every time I saw him appear in the doorway and come my way again. I had expected him to be aloof and spend most of the time lounging in the master bedroom like I'd be doing in his position, but I felt more like a houseguest.

I might have been a houseguest who happens to like flirting with him every now and then, but a houseguest nonetheless.

Later in the morning, once everything was set up to my satisfaction for the time being, I headed inside and came in through the back door to the kitchen, wiping the sweat from my brow with a rag I carried in my truck. A strange sound met me when I opened the door, and I looked over to see Jesse standing over a blender just before turning it off and looking over his shoulder at me.

"Ah, damn—I was about to surprise you," he said affably as he lifted the blender with a purple-colored substance in and poured the thick drink into two tall glasses. "It's not exactly a pile of eggs and sausage, but I think it's pretty tasty. If not, I won't be offended if you want to hit a diner on your own later," he added.

I approached and took one of the glasses, peered at it apprehensively as Jesse watched with anticipation, and I took a long drink out of it. A sweet burst of flavor washed the coffee taste out of my mouth, and the cold was the exact kind of refreshing I needed.

"I haven't actually made a breakfast smoothie before, so let me know if it tastes like sawdust or something," he said modestly as he picked up the empty pitcher and rinsed it out in the sink.

I wanted to tell him to see for himself, grab him by the waist, spin him around, and plant a deep kiss on his lips that would let him do just that. The visual appeared in my head so strongly that when Jesse met my gaze, I thought he could almost read my mind. But were we there yet? We had only just agreed that last night wasn't a massive breach of professional trust. Jesse seemed to like me flirting with him as much as I liked it, no matter how slowly I wanted to take it, but I didn't want to make him feel like I was taking advantage of him.

"Delicious," I said, sliding his glass toward him. "Blueberry, blackberry, banana...and coconut?"

"Close," he said triumphantly, "coconut *milk*. L.A. might be an easy place to lose yourself, but one thing they're not short on is health food. I just... wasn't that good at getting into it," he admitted sheepishly. "It's a great milk substitute if you don't mind the undercurrent of coconut. Otherwise, cashew milk is closest to the taste and texture of actual milk."

I had to admit, I never thought I'd say this, but something vegan wasn't half-bad.

"This would be good for a refresher when you're outdoors all day," I said, leaning against the counter as Jesse took his first sip of his breakfast. "And I was thinking, since I'm here and you're wanting to get active, why don't we hit the lake next time we get a chance? There's some bad weather blowing in over the next few days, but I have my old canoe at my mom's house from back in high school, and as far as I know, it's still in good shape. It's a two-person, so it doesn't matter if you've never been canoeing before. I'll make sure you don't fall into the water. Good way to burn some calories and get back to old times all at once."

"That sounds like a dream," Jesse said enthusiastically.

"Just one condition: pack one of these for each of us," I said, holding up my glass to him, and he laughed.

"Deal," he said, clinking his glass to mine.

JESSE

THE RAIN PELTED THE GLOSSY, WIDE BAY WINDOW AS THE THICK GRAY clouds knitted themselves together tightly across the sky. It was only early afternoon, but it looked dark enough outside to be much later in the day. Although I was sure most of the residents of Winchester were probably grumbling and complaining about the inclement weather, I had a different take on it. I had spent so much time living in Los Angeles that I actually got kind of excited for stormy, rainy days. In L.A., the sunshine was relentless. It was good for my moods most of the time, and I was fully aware of what a privilege it was to live in a place where it was basically eternally summertime. But I wasn't from Los Angeles originally, and sometimes I missed a good rainy day. It encouraged you to stay inside, which could be a good or a bad thing depending on whether you wanted to go out and get things done. I was enjoying the excuse to stay inside though and not bother with the pouring rain beyond the walls of the lake house. There was a sleepy, cozy feeling to the afternoon. This was what a friend of mine back in Los Angeles often called "nap weather." She was right. I couldn't stop yawning, my brain inevitably wandering back to fantasize about how soft and cushy my bed upstairs would be if I just abandoned my current activity and gave in to the overwhelming desire to curl up under the sheets and waste the day away.

But I was determined to make every day of my time here in Winchester count. I knew there would be plenty of time to rest and relax, which was another thing I had come all the way out here to do. After all, it was in large part due to my grueling, nonstop work schedule back home that I had fallen out of shape and let myself go a little bit. I had simply never been able to find the time or energy to take a long walk or go for a swim in one of the private pools in my gated neighborhood. By the time I had finished a sixteen-hour day of hastily memorizing lines, redoing the same emotionally charged scene over and over again with the camera crew gazing at my face from every conceivable angle, and fielding calls, texts, and emails relayed to me by my agent, any desire to exercise had flown out the window. At the end of a long filming day, all I wanted to do was collapse into bed, go low-grade comatose for six hours, and then get up early to head into hair and makeup to start the whole shebang over again. It was great fun, and I was eternally grateful for the fact that I had such an exciting, rewarding job. But truthfully, it could be a little isolating sometimes. It was easy to get caught up in the back-to-back days locked up on a sound stage with my costars and a massive film crew and forget to take care of myself in the little downtime I had. And when every day was bright, warm, and sunny, it was even more difficult to justify staying in bed and relaxing.

Which was why I felt pretty okay with the past five days of rainy, gray weather here in Winchester. It forced me to stay in, alternating between relaxation and exercise. Currently, I was briskly working out on an elliptical machine positioned in the downstairs study so that I could get a lovely view of the rainy, foggy lake while I burned calories. A thick mist was rolling out over the still, peaceful waters. The sky above was so dark and gray, it reflected onto the lake and made it look nearly black. The trees in the backyard leading down to the water's edge were softly swaying in the wind as rain pelted their leaves and made them shiny and slick. The wooden dock that reached out into the lake was soaked with rainwater, turning it a dark, dense brown.

The two-person canoe moored to the dock swayed from side to side in the soft current and rain. It sat lower in the water than usual, as it was heavy with rainwater. Yesterday I had noticed that and panicked for a moment, thinking it might actually get too full of water and start sinking. But a bemused Marshall had calmly explained to me that it would be fine, and that it was meant to withstand a large amount of water collecting in the hollows.

"Phew." I sighed, shaking my head slightly as I worked out on the elliptical.

My thighs and calves were burning, which normally would mark the point at which I would give up on exercising. But Marshall had insisted that the burn was a good thing. That it was my body's muscles breaking down and releasing lactic acid as a result of a vigorous workout. He'd explained that it was good to reach the point of burning, then push a little further, and then cool down to a stop. I was pushing myself right now, trying to burn as many calories as possible in a short amount of time. Perhaps it was the perfectionist in me, but I wanted to constantly be improving, pushing further and further each time. I knew it was important to take time to relax and let my muscles heal up in between workouts, but I couldn't help but want to accelerate the process. It was my natural tendency. It made me one hell of a reliable actor, but it could get me into trouble in situations that required more patience than dogged determination. I wanted to get things done right away, as quickly as possible. That was probably another reason why my fitness had gotten out of hand. I didn't want to spend the time necessary to get back into shape. I wanted to get it all over and done with immediately rather than taking my time. But luckily, I wasn't alone in this. I had the best, most patient guide of all: Marshall.

The other day, Marshall had turned up with his truck packed with expensive exercise equipment. None of the equipment was especially shiny or new, but it was good quality stuff. Perhaps unsurprisingly, Marshall just happened to own all of these workout machines. I assumed he had collected them over the years as a means of buffing up his physique to better handle his job as a door guy at The Chisel.

Once I'd laid eyes on the equipment he'd carried into the lake house piece by piece, it all had made sense. No wonder he was so strong and capable—he had all the necessary tools at hand! I was grateful to him for moving all his workout gear into the house, and I even felt a little touched that he had taken my confession about wanting to get back into shape to heart. He was stony-faced and quiet, but I was quickly learning that his reticence was no indicator that he wasn't listening. In fact, I had not even known Marshall very long yet, and I already felt as though he listened to me more intently than anyone else I had ever known. He was so genuine, so real. There was never any pretense about who he was and what he wanted. No games. No shade. Just bespoke good-heartedness and country-boy toughness. In my opinion, that was one hell of a package, especially when I compared him to most of the guys I knew back in Los Angeles. I adored L.A., of course, but I wasn't naïve enough not to notice the fact that people tended to be a little... flaky. Everyone talked over one another. Everyone was constantly vibrating with the desire to speak their mind and talk about themselves. It was a self-centered, gossipy culture that could be great fun most of the time if you were realistic about your expectations, but I had to admit that it was a nice change to deal with some truly authentic people. Winchester locals seemed more likely to speak their mind, not out of a desire to theatrically claim the spotlight, but because they valued honesty as a virtue rather than just an opportunity to talk about themselves.

Then again, maybe I was a little biased. After all, the only Winchesterite I had been interacting with lately was Marshall, and he was truly amazing. If the rest of the people in this town were even a fraction as kind, patient, and steadfast as Marshall, they were good folks.

I was excited to keep up my new workout routine with his guidance, maybe even moving on to some of the more inscrutable equipment I didn't understand yet. So far, I had stuck to the tried-and-true cardio equipment, running on the treadmill and stepping on the elliptical. I had even attempted some stretches that were not quite yoga, not quite Pilates. More like yoga-adjacent. My legs pretty much constantly ached these past few days, and it felt as though my abdominal muscles were slowly waking up from a years-long hibernation. It had been quite some time since I last saw myself with the kind of rock-hard, well-defined abs I boasted of in my youth. I wasn't dramatically overweight. In fact, in most social circles I would be looked at as totally ordinary. But Los Angeles was a different story. People there kind of graded your physical beauty on a sharp curve. So many inhabitants of Hollywood were beyond gorgeous: stick-thin with flawless skin, teeth, and hair. Models and actresses owned the streets. Perfect faces and bodies were splashed across gigantic billboards that were impossible to ignore. Everywhere you looked, you saw people walking around with almost no body fat, with physiques that were so expertly sculpted as to look almost fake.

We were all trying to adjust for the ten pounds the camera added, whether it was a conscious effort or not. If that meant spending every free moment engaged in hardcore exercise and never, ever indulging in a lie-in or some piping-hot, crispy churros from the vendor down the street from the film set... then so be it.

But it wasn't like that here. People enjoyed their food. People used food to show appreciation, love and support. It was an opportunity to bond with your fellow man. It was a ritual, a tradition that brought families and friends and even strangers together for the same purpose. Instead of furtively sneaking a side salad at brunch because you knew you had an audition the next day and you wanted to be as slim as possible, people just ate what they wanted. Winchester folks weren't all massively overweight either—they just naturally seemed to know the right balance. It was impressive to me, coming from a town of high-strung, hyperconscious eaters.

Also impressive, as well as confusing, were the complicated pieces of equipment Marshall had brought over. Particularly the ones meant for strength training. That was something I had never done because in all honesty, people in L.A. cared more about how strong and fit you looked rather than how strong and fit you actually were. Casting agents were looking for a toned body, not a body that could bench-press the entire crew. It was all optics. All for show.

Marshall was refreshing in that way. He not only looked tough—

he *was* tough. And he was never a braggart about it, even though he totally could have been. The accolades were absolutely warranted with this guy. I felt completely secure in the knowledge that he was my bodyguard. I knew he was strong enough. I knew he was cautious enough. He was detail-oriented, the kind of man who never missed a thing. And damn, was he a hard worker. In fact, right now, as I slowed down the pace on the elliptical machine, Marshall was out in the rain, working on setting up security tools around the property. The rain didn't seem to bother him one bit. He was unfazeable.

However, there was something weighing rather heavily on my mind. But I couldn't tell if it was burdening Marshall to the same extent, if at all. He was so stoic, so adept at keeping his face unreadable and his tone so even-keeled it was impressive. Nothing seemed to ruffle his feathers, not even the fact that he and I had engaged in some particularly unprofessional behavior together days ago. We still had not discussed what had happened. I had a feeling we were both waiting for the other to bring it up, both too uneasy to mention it ourselves and risk rocking the boat. That was understandable. We clearly had a fantastic working dynamic, and neither of us wanted to do anything that might jeopardize that. Marshall had made it clear he wasn't bothered or distressed by what we had done, but beyond that, any deeper discussion of what it might mean for us going forward had dropped off completely. We got along so well without even having to try, and it was scary to imagine bringing up what had happened between us and put that great relationship at risk. I was privileged and happy to have Marshall around, both as a bodyguard and as a low-key fitness guide, and I was afraid of losing that if I pushed the issue too far. At the same time, though, I knew we would have to talk about it sometime. It was inevitable. We were both pretty skilled at avoidance maneuvers, but with how much time we'd be spending together, it would bound to come up again sometime. Right?

Just as I was finishing my workout, the cooldown phase coming to an end, I heard the front door click open and shut again. I turned off the elliptical machine and stepped off, my chest heaving slightly with the effort. I was sweaty all over, a fact I hadn't really realized until now. I suddenly felt self-conscious, and it was no puzzle to figure out why.

Marshall kicked off his boots at the door. He was dressed in his usual fare plus a glossy raincoat covered with glistening drops of water. His cheeks were flushed a deep, ruddy red, his eyes looking even sharper and brighter than usual. He looked every bit the part of a grizzled, competent mountain man, and I found myself irresistibly attracted to the look. I swallowed back my arousal and forced a smile.

"How'd it go?" I asked, swiping some of the sweat from my forehead.

"Good. Wet," he said. "All the security cams are hooked up now. I should have a clear, unobstructed view from all angles of the property."

"Wow. That's impressive," I said, letting out a low whistle.

"You want to take a look?" he offered, shrugging off his raincoat and hanging it on the coat rack by the door.

"Sure! Just, uh, let me get cleaned up first," I said hastily.

"Go for it," Marshall replied.

I rushed upstairs to the master bedroom, closing the door behind me and peeling off my sweaty clothes on the way into the en suite. I flicked on the light and started the shower, letting it heat up while I looked at myself in the mirror. My face was flushed, too, and beaded with sweat. It was a look I had only rarely seen on myself. I kind of liked it.

I hopped into the shower and quickly rinsed off, emerging afterward like a brand-new man. I put on some comfortable, casual clothing and headed back downstairs to find Marshall. He was sitting in the sun-room with his laptop on the glass coffee table. He was hunched over the keyboard, peering intently at the screen. The laptop was a normal size, but it looked almost comically small compared to Marshall. I fought back a smile of amusement as I walked in and took a seat beside him, taking care to keep several inches between us just for courtesy's sake. On the screen were several small rectangles, all displaying a different angle of the lake house property. I couldn't help but be amazed.

"Wow. You really chose the best locations for these cams, Marshall," I told him.

He nodded. "Took a little finagling, but we got it. There are motion sensors connected to the cameras, too, so if we get any movement on the property, it'll catch it. If the cameras snap a photo of the culprit, it sends the picture directly to my phone. That way I'll always have a beat on what's going on around here, even if I'm not physically present for whatever reason," he explained to me.

"So if that obnoxious paparazzo shows up again...?" I trailed off.

He nodded slowly. "I'll know about it and put a stop to it," he said, a rare smiling brightening his sharp features. I felt my heart skip a beat.

"You seem really happy about that," I remarked.

"I like doing my job well, and having eyes on every part of the property lets me do that. Plus, you know I like keeping an eye on you. I like knowing you're safe, Jesse. It's a good feeling," he said in a quieter voice.

By now, I felt like I might melt through the sofa and the floor. I looked at him sidelong, my heart racing as the words gradually formed in my mouth.

"You know... I have to admit I've had a hard time keeping you out of my head these past several days," I began softly. "You're all I can think about. I don't want to risk our working relationship, Marshall, but I have to be honest. Have you given any more thought to what happened between us last week?"

He turned to face me, a bright fire flashing in his eyes that sent an electrical current running down my spine. Marshall's perfect, sensual lips parted, and he said the words I wanted but never expected to hear: "It's been on my mind constantly. It's all I can think about."

And a mere moment later, before I could even respond, he pounced on me.

MARSHALL

It hadn't just been on my mind; it had been taking every ounce of my strength to keep my hands off Jesse this entire time. Whenever I had heard him stirring in the bedroom next to me at night, it made me grow hard between my legs and crave the feeling of his lips again. Every time I heard his voice, I wanted to hear it sighing with desire for me. I wanted to maintain a professional distance, wanted to play it safe, but I couldn't put it off anymore. My hunger for Jesse was going to consume me if I didn't reach out and take him.

That was exactly what I did.

If someone had told me a week ago that this was where my interview with Jesse was going to lead me, I would have laughed it off. It didn't have anything to do with the fact that Jesse was a man. That part was still new, but it was the kind of new that gave me a rush for life I didn't want to stop. But Jesse and I didn't make sense, I thought. I was the kind of guy that guys like him had watching their door, not watching them undress.

We came from similar worlds, but our lives now couldn't be more different. And yet we kept finding subtle ways our feelings intersected, somehow. It wasn't just Jesse's body I desired. I wanted something more, something closer to that feeling I got every time I realized this was someone I might be able to open up to.

Still holding Jesse to me, I walked him back until he bumped against the cool glass of the sunroom's window pane walls. Outside, the pouring rain was dumping cascades of water over the beautiful glass room that distorted the view from outside. This was definitely not the first day of rain after a dry spell, so I wasn't worried about flash floods. All I was worried about was getting caught... even if some part of me found that exciting.

Getting caught in the act with this guy who was so hot I could have sworn the glass was already fogging up was an exciting idea. It would have been a career-ending idea, too, but we wanted this, and I was way past the point of denying what I couldn't live without. Nothing short of Jesse's refusal would stop me now.

But the rain was so heavy that it practically formed a curtain of water that distorted all visibility both ways. Even as my body pinned him against the glass and pushed my hips against his, feeling his chest swell up in a silent gasp, I knew that all anyone would be able to see from outside was the vague, warbling shapes that I could see from the inside.

My cock was already hard from just those few seconds of touching him. I couldn't remember the last time I had been so drawn to someone, so ignited, like it wasn't prepared to have been this restrained around someone I wanted like this. My hands found his, and I held them for a moment before finally breaking the kiss and grabbing his hips.

My mouth went to his ear, letting him feel and hear the hungry breath I let out as I ground our hips together and groped his ass. I had to restrain myself because my idea of gentle was not the same as most people's. A greedy squeeze of his ass showed him my strength, but not all of it. He felt my shaft brush against his, but only for a moment.

And every time I teased him like that, I felt his body mirroring mine, trying to follow me and feel more of what I had to offer. His hands drifted down my sides, feeling my muscles one by one on their way to my wrists. But when he reached my waist, I reached down, took him by the wrists, and pinned them against the glass above his head and looked him in the eye, swiping my tongue over my lips.

"I want to pick up where we left off," I growled, absolutely no ambiguity in my voice. "I want to take you, Jesse. No holds barred. You have to give me the green light for that. I'm not going to hold back."

"I do," he breathed, nodding. "I just want to be sure you do."

I kissed him on the neck, a fierce and possessive kiss I wanted to use to drive away his worries. I sucked on his skin and smelled his subtle cologne, squeezing his ass and showing him just how much I craved him.

"You have no idea how hard it is, sleeping in that bed and knowing you're right there, just a wall away," I growled, reaching up and running a hand through his hair.

"Show me how you want it to be," he challenged me, and something about that hint of defiance in his voice set my skin on fire.

I reached down to the hem of his shirt and pulled it up over his head, exposing him to me and watching me drink in the sight of his torso. There was worry in his eyes, and I knew it was because Jesse wasn't comfortable with how he looked.

No matter. I would just have to prove to him how much I liked every inch of what I saw.

I bent my knees and slid my hands under his ass, not just to feel him up, but this time, to pick him up. He yelped and threw his arms around me to hold on as I chuckled and carried him to the large couch in the middle of the room. It was a spacious, cozy sitting area where I'd watched him sitting with a tall glass of water and a book in his hands at least a dozen times. Each time, I'd wanted to pin him down on it, and now, I finally had the chance.

I set him down on the couch and pushed him flat on his back before I stripped off my shirt and watched the color rising in his cheeks. Before he could squirm away, I threw a leg over his waist and straddled him, but my body was so big that one of my legs was still on the ground. I didn't mind that one bit. In fact, there was something thrilling about feeling like I was overwhelming Jesse with my frame, making him feel small and controlled. Half the pleasure was the fact that he so clearly seemed to like it.

I cradled his head with one hand and leaned down to kiss him before wandering further down his body. I felt his shoulders and sensed the muscle under the soft give of his skin, and I brought my lips down to it. My mouth followed my hands as I kissed all over his chest, breathing on it and groping it as I went.

"Don't you get shy around me," I growled to drive my point home.

Part of me wanted to assure him that I wanted to feel his body no matter what its size. I wanted to tell him I thought he was perfect the way he was, and that I was about to make this body feel just as good as it would in any figure. But I didn't even want his mind on that subject right now. Nothing needed to get in the way of us, not while the rain was on our side, shutting out all the noisy thoughts swarming my mind.

There was just us, and I was going to take full advantage of that.

Under my attention, I felt Jesse's body slowly start to relax. I felt it in a deep breath of his at first, and bit by bit, I felt less tension throughout his body. He shivered when I brought my face down to the outline of his cock bulging through his pants. But I didn't touch it. Instead, I looked up at him slowly, a ravenous smile spreading across my face.

Jesse groaned as I took off his belt and opened his pants, and as soon as they were loose, I grasped the waist and pulled them down to his knees in one swift motion, along with his underwear. The moment I laid eyes on the stiff, thick cock that bobbed free, I felt overwhelmed by my instincts. After ripping his pants the rest of the way off him, I descended.

One knee went to the left of his hip while I bent down to kiss him and wrap my right hand around his cock, massaging it hungrily as soon as our lips touched. Jesse gasped, but it turned into a half-shuddering sigh as his body melted in my grasp. He pushed his hips forward, and I grasped his hair with one hand to keep his neck exposed and let me kiss it, too.

I felt something on my belt as my thumb started sweeping over the tip of Jesse's swollen crown, and I realized that Jesse was trying to take his turn working my pants off. I turned my hips inward to give him a better angle, and soon, he had my belt undone and was trying to keep a grip on the buttons that held the denim together just next to my fully erect cock.

When he almost had one of the buttons open, I tightened my grip on his cock just enough to surprise him with a wave of pleasure that rolled through his shaft and up to his groin. It distracted him enough to let his hand slip, and I did the same thing a few buttons later. I heard him laugh softly this time as he caught on, and in return, he brought one of his hands to the tip of my bulging outline and squeezed it just enough to make me feel it. Maybe I had felt a little guilty for teasing him at first, but Jesse liked to tease back.

He got my jeans open in just a few moments, despite me having my fun, and I helped him work them down my thighs. Like me, he must not have been able to stop himself from feeling my manhood from tip to base as soon as it was exposed. I kicked off the pants and straddled Jesse again, pressing his cock to mine and looking down at the gorgeous face gazing up at mine.

I wasn't the kind of guy who saw any use in bragging, but the way my fully stiff shaft was lying on Jesse's and taking up so much space on his crotch put a look on Jesse's face that made me proud of my entire body's size. He was intimidated by me, but he wanted me, and he might have even wanted me more because of how naturally and easily I could overwhelm him.

On some level, I thought it made him feel... safe. Stunning good looks aside, Jesse was a strong man with a good, solid frame, and I was one of few men who could look down on him in the first place. But he seemed to relax around me, and the thought of holding him in my arms and making him feel secure fanned a hot-burning flame within me.

"Do you want to let me in, Jesse?" I asked with a gruff rumble.

"I want you to show me what you can do," Jesse moaned softly as he reached for our cocks and wrapped his hand around both of them as well as he could, "so I can show you everything *I* can do."

I sucked in a sharp breath as he used his warm, soft hand to pump both of our shafts together, base to tip, perfectly shaped fingers dancing their way across our cocks and sending a burst of pleasure up my body. I felt the muscles around my hips stretching and loosening as nicely as the first stretch after a good night's sleep, and it melted into tension that welled up in my crotch.

I let out a deep groan, rolling my shoulders back and letting my mouth hang open as I gazed down at Jesse and devoured him with my eyes. The spark in his eye when he looked at me and our cocks made me want him all the more, and I had to focus to keep control of myself as he touched me. I felt his cock pulse against mine, and mine stiffened even more in response. A wonderful shiver rippled through me, and after swiping my thumb over Jesse's lower lip, I brought the hand behind us.

"I have to admit," I growled, "I've never wanted a man before like I want you, but fuck, I can't keep my hands off you."

Before he could reply, I stretched my arm to bring my finger to his hole. He tensed, then relaxed with a delighted sigh as I swirled my fingertip around him, feeling how tight he was. The thought of sliding my cock into that excited me. It had never crossed my mind before meeting Jesse that I could be so into a man. I didn't care. It was laughable to me that anyone *could* care. Anyone who thought that way never felt the way I felt about Jesse right then.

A smile crossed my face at the feeling of his cock twitching every time my finger found a spot that made him squirm under me. I took my time with him, smug that I had shown him that even though he's the one holding our cocks, I was in control. He was a willing captive between my thighs, and I knew how to hold the reins of his stunning body.

I felt wetness on the bottom of my cock, and I looked down to see Jesse's hand pass over a sheen of his precome. My eyes drifted up to his face, and I saw him blushing, biting his lip as he looked up at me.

"Condom?" I asked.

"Nightstand in the master bedroom," he breathed. "With the lube."

He started to get up to get it, but I stopped him with the same motion I used to stop him from getting up at the restaurant the first time we touched. I winked and went to grab the items and was back in half a minute. After applying both of them, I stood before Jesse, whose legs were still parted for me.

I crossed my arms over my chest and smiled down at him judiciously. He stopped running his hand up and down his shaft and peered up at me searchingly, probably wondering what I was thinking.

My balls felt swollen and sore. At last, I spoke in a husky growl, thick with desire, "Get on your knees."

Jesse's blush grew at my tone, and I saw goose bumps on his arms before he obeyed and turned around, grasping a pillow and arm of the couch while arching his back to present his backside to me.

Jesse's ass was smooth and round, and my cock ached at the sight of it. I wanted to bury my manhood deep inside him, but I had to restrain my instincts and be patient. I reached out to grasp his cheeks, and I pushed forward as I pulled him back. My crown and his hole touched, and as they slipped around each other, I felt pure bliss.

My body had never reacted like this to sex. I thought I knew everything about what I liked, but Jesse proved me very, very wrong. And for once, I was glad to be wrong.

I rocked my hips back and forth slowly, feeling waves upon waves of burning pleasure through my body as I felt Jesse moving in time with me. Our rhythm started slow and steady. I was big, and sometimes, I felt like I might break Jesse if I weren't careful. But as I gained depth and felt more of his warmth around me, I picked up the pace, and Jesse met me at every thrust. The man was anything but passive in all ways, it seemed.

Soon, my cock pumped into him with a steady, piston-like rhythm. Whenever one of our bodies started to move differently, the other found a way to follow in perfect timing. I reached around his waist and found his shaft, and as soon as I did, I worked his shaft like he had done to ours just a moment ago. But my hand was a lot bigger, and I took special pleasure in covering as much of his cock as I could with every stroke. I even reached further down to let the tips of my fingers feel his aching balls that were just begging to be released.

"I might be your bodyguard," I growled as I felt myself edging closer to the edge of release, "but right now, you're *mine*."

I felt Jesse's balls tightening as he breathed a ragged gasp, and I let my tension snap and boil over at last. Hot fluid shot from my cock before I even felt the first pulse shake me like never before, almost paralyzing me in this electric trance of hard, blissful rhythms, and the sweet feeling of Jesse's cock coming in my hand.

The sound of our deep panting mixed with the steady downpour outside, and while my cock twitched and released its last come in Jesse, I beamed down at him with a flushed face. Then something else caught my eye—I looked up at the windows that made up the ceiling to see a tiny gap in the clouds, and the afternoon sun was peeking through it just enough to cast a beam of sunlight across the floor of the room. I felt a sense of utter calm wash over me, and I slowly slipped out of Jesse, who slid to the side, where I could see the smile on his panting face before he looked up at me.

"Hey," he said, smile widening.

"Hey," I replied, unable to hold back a chuckle, and I leaned down to scoop him up in my arms and kiss him.

He sighed into me, and the sound carried so much simple satisfaction with it that my heart soared.

"That was... unbelievable," I admitted, smiling down at him with lidded eyes.

"I completely agree," he said, pecking me on the cheek. "Sky's clearing up," he pointed out, nodding above me.

"Probably means we should get out of here and clean up," I said with a grin.

"Probably," he admitted, still blushing and glowing like a sunset on the beach, and he paused before continuing. "And hey, since we might as well hit the en suite shower...want to crash with me tonight?"

I chuckled and planted a soft kiss to his lips.

"I'd like that," I growled. "And this time, I'll be there in the morning...even if you sleep in."

He laughed and pecked me on the cheek, and we hurried out of the sun-room before the rain thinned enough to let the world see what we had gotten up to. But as we left, I noticed that might not have even been necessary.

The panes were smattered with a thin layer of fog.

JESSE

It was a gorgeous day here in Winchester. After nearly a full week of almost constant downpours and gray skies, the sun had finally re-emerged from its hibernation behind the clouds and was shining in full force, casting the lakefront property in beautiful, uplifting light. The heavy rains had stimulated a new wave of growth in the myriad species of flora growing all around the lake house. The grass was a deeper, lusher green. The tiny wild strawberries were plump and red and juicy-looking, even though they were still small enough to hold several of them in the palm of one's hand. Everywhere I looked, there were wild flowers sprouting through the grass, curling and bending enthusiastically toward the new sun.

As I looked out the back windows of the sun-room, it seemed as though a thick carpeting of multicolored flowers had appeared out of nowhere, a dense carpeting of rainbow colors. Butterflies and buzzing honeybees flitted from petal to petal, busily making up for lost time. Outside the kitchen window that let the sun shine brilliantly in on the massive garden sink was a thick, tall cluster of hydrangeas which bloomed in gorgeous hues of blue, green, pink, and purple. There was a red nectar-feeder hanging from a thin metal post in the midst of the blooms, which attracted tiny, iridescent hummingbirds with their long, sharp beaks and their tiny feet. I saw all manner of birds and small woodland critters fluttering and scurrying around the property, as though all of them were newly inspired to action by the emergence of the long-lost sunshine.

I'd awoken this morning to the most beautiful sight of all: Marshall lying next to me in bed, his eyes shut and his chest slowly rising and falling in perfect tempo. Even asleep, he looked intimidating, as though I had stumbled across a resting stone giant who could come thundering back to life at any moment. But seeing him like this still made my heart melt. I propped myself up on my elbow slowly and cautiously so as not to wake him, hoping to squeeze in a few moments of just watching him sleep. Was it creepy? Maybe a little. But I couldn't help myself. My eyes followed the sharp curve of his cheek-bones, down the barely visible bump on the bridge of his nose, along the heavy, cut line of his jaw. I let my gaze linger for a moment on his soft lips, slightly parted so that he could breathe rhythmically in and out. His dark hair was adorably tousled, and I found myself licking my lips at the hint of his naked, perfect body underneath the sheets. I was torn in half trying to decide which was better: letting him sleep so I could admire him a while longer or gently waking him up with soft kisses and warm words.

Before I could make a decision, though, his gorgeous eyes fluttered open and blinked a few times, looking at me. Immediately, my face began to burn and I couldn't help but grin sheepishly. He looked so incredibly handsome with his messy hair and the sunlight filtering through over his flawless skin and stubble-rough jawline. Although his lips did not upturn into a smile, I could see the smile in his eyes.

"G'morning," he grunted hoarsely.

"Good morning," I replied.

"What time is it?" he asked.

I turned over to glance at the alarm clock, then grimaced.

"Ten to ten," I revealed.

"Damn," he groaned. "I haven't slept in this late in years."

"Years?" I repeated incredulously, turning back to Marshall.

He chuckled, a sound that made my heart beat faster. "Yes. I'm usually up and at 'em by eight thirty at the latest. You must have really tired me out," he remarked suggestively.

My blush deepened. "Same to you," I said.

Marshall yawned and pulled himself up into a sitting position, ruffling his fingers through his thick, dark hair. He squinted toward the window and said, "Wow. The sun's back. I'd almost forgotten what it looked like."

"I know. It looks like it's going to be a gorgeous day," I agreed.

"That gives me an idea, actually," he said. "We ought to take advantage of the good weather now that it's here."

"What's on your mind?" I asked eagerly.

"The lake looks calm. I'm thinking we pack up a lunch and head out on the water for some canoeing and do some exploring. I think there's supposed to be some hidden little island out there on Lake Wren somewhere," he mused aloud.

"A hidden island?" I said, smiling widely. "Sounds like something a kid would dream up for kicks to me."

Marshall shrugged. "That could be true. But what better opportunity to hunt down a potentially-made-up place than a day like this?" he reasoned.

"Good point. It'll be a good time either way," I said, nodding.

Marshall slid out of bed and stretched. I watched, my mouth nearly watering at the sight of his taut ass and the rippling muscles of his broad, powerful back and biceps. He was naked and not at all ashamed or self-conscious, which only made it even hotter. I wondered if I could ever get to a point where I felt as confident with my body as he was.

He walked into the en suite and, just before he disappeared inside the bathroom, he poked his head out of the doorway and remarked, "I'm going to shower off if you want to join."

I could hardly get out of bed fast enough.

We stood under the water together, chatting a little as we lathered up and rinsed off. I couldn't tell which factor was more helpful for waking me up: the hot, steamy water or the hot, steamy guy I was sharing it with. Either way, we managed to keep our hands to ourselves. Afterward, we quickly toweled off and got dressed in casual shorts, T-shirts, and sandals before heading into the kitchen to make coffee and prepare some lunches to take with us on our Lake Wren adventure. We made sandwiches with sliced tomato, cucumber, avocado, spicy mustard, Havarti cheese, and some delicious honey-roasted turkey breast Marshall had procured from a local butcher. Even the mustard came from a Winchester artisan who stone ground the stuff herself. I was continually impressed with how well-rounded and talented the people of Winchester were. They all seemed to put so much effort, heart, and soul into their work, which I greatly admired. We tossed in a couple snack-sized bags of baked chips and two giant thermoses of water, and we were off.

As we carried the lunch cooler down to the dock, I couldn't help but marvel at the beautiful surroundings. Birds twittered cheerily in the tree branches, and I saw no less than six butterflies just on the walk from the back deck down to the water's edge.

"Damn, I forgot how nice the sun feels on my skin," I sighed happily.

"Couldn't ask for better weather than this," Marshall added as he tipped the canoe to get the rainwater out.

I climbed in the front of the canoe, got situated, then held onto the dock with one hand to keep the canoe steady. Then Marshall put down the cooler in front of me, half under the bow, untied the rope from the wooden post, and carefully sat on the seat behind me. We grabbed our respective oars, pushed off, and paddled at a leisurely pace while the waves gently rocked the canoe. We were in no hurry today, both of us more interested in getting some vitamin D and enjoying the adventure. For a while we paddled in relative silence, content to soak up the sun. But once we got a little farther out and the dock was starting to disappear from view, Marshall suddenly struck up a conversation I had not expected to hear.

"So, it looks like I'm going to have to reconfigure my assumptions about my own sexuality," he said matter-of-factly.

I blinked with surprise at the new topic and turned my head to

Marshall. "Oh. Okay. Really?" I said, stunned. I quickly turned back when the canoe began to wobble precariously.

He nodded, looking contemplative but not remotely bothered. "I've always kind of thought of myself as straight. But then again, I've never really tested that out all the way."

"So what are you thinking now?" I asked. I was a little anxious about the answer. I couldn't see him with my back to him, but by the slight jerking motion of the canoe, I could feel him shrug.

"Well, I sure enjoy what we do together. I have no regrets, and I know I would like to do it again sometime. I don't think it really needs a whole lot more thought than that," he surmised.

"Huh. That's a pretty New Age-y way to look at it," I teased.

He laughed, a gorgeous sound that made me feel all warm and fuzzy inside.

"Maybe so. I don't mind it. I'll admit I don't usually contemplate my feelings too deeply, but I know what I like and I know what I want, and that's good enough for now," he explained sagely.

"That seems pretty logical," I agreed. "Although I have a different outlook on the whole thing, admittedly. I've known I was gay for a long, long time. Never felt like I needed to change myself or hide it, really. It's just part of who I am, but it's not *all* that I am, you know?"

"I get you," Marshall said. "So I assume that means you must have dated your fair share of men, then?"

I laughed. "Well, it hasn't exactly been a revolving door of men in my life if that's what you're picturing, but yeah. I've dated. Nothing too serious. My career has always been more important to me than anything in my personal life, for better or for worse," I said.

He nodded slowly. "I can definitely relate to that. I think I just try to stay busy. Keeps my mind from wandering off to places it shouldn't go," he said.

"It's an easy trap to fall into," I sighed. "Putting work before everything else."

"I agree. I'd be lying if I said I didn't often lean on my work to keep me distracted from other things," Marshall quipped.

"So, how long have you been in the security business?" I asked, prodding for more information.

I couldn't help it. I was so intrigued by Marshall I wanted to know everything there was to know about him.

"Well, I've always been a big guy. Back when I was a kid growing up here in Winchester, I was the default kid who stuck up for the little guys. It seemed only natural to lean into that and kind of make it my whole life. I've always liked defending those who couldn't defend themselves. I have a cousin who is a few years younger than me. He was really sick for a while as a kid, so he's always been a little scrawny compared to me. The bullies used to pick on him because he was small, because they knew he was ill. But when he was a freshman in high school, I was a senior. That's when the bullying came to a halt. I caught those jerks trying to shove my cousin into a garbage can behind the gymnasium, and I saw red," he recalled.

"Wow. What happened?" I asked.

"Now, I'm not exactly proud of this, but let's just say the whole lot of them ended up in the nurse's office, and I ended up in detention. The principal even warned me that if it ever happened again, he wouldn't let me walk across the stage at graduation. But it was worth it. Those losers never messed with my cousin again," he said.

I dared a backward glance just in time to see his confident smirk. God, he was hot as hell.

"Damn. That's impressive," I said truthfully. "I was never like that as a kid. I didn't get picked on, luckily, but I was no tough guy either. This probably won't come as a surprise, but I was pretty involved with the theater department growing up."

"You don't say?" Marshall teased playfully.

"It's true," I said, laughing. "I've always been a ham for the camera since day one."

"No wonder you ended up in show biz," he remarked.

"Yeah. Los Angeles was always my goal as a youth growing up in rural Tennessee. I remember watching *Bannister Heights* with my mom as a teen, believe it or not. I never imagined I would star in the reboot. It's all been such a whirlwind, you know?" I mused.

"My mom watches it religiously," Marshall said. "It's her guilty pleasure. I bet it's a lot of fun working on it."

"It is. Lots of work. Long hours. But definitely a good time. My costars are fantastic, and there are some seriously talented writers who keep the ratings in the stratosphere. I've been very fortunate," I said. "Though I will say there's a dark side to the fame and constant pressure. If I'm not filming, I'm attending galas and premieres and late-night parties. Anything and everything to stay relevant and informed. I know that probably sounds shallow, but it's the way things tend to work in L.A."

"I get it. You have to be a part of the rat race whether you want to or not. It was kind of like that in Atlanta, too. Missing a staff party or event could be a big problem for my career, so I ended up attending a lot of events I really didn't want to go to," Marshall shared.

"And then there's the fact that I've kind of lost steady contact with my family," I sighed. "I feel the worst about that. My family has always been totally supportive and caring. I owe my success to their support, for sure. But I've just been so busy lately that I guess I got caught up in it and let those relationships slide a little. Don't get me wrong—I love living in Los Angeles. I love my job. But sometimes I feel a little disconnected from my roots."

"Me, too. Being away from Winchester for a decade has changed me. Sometimes I feel like I don't quite fit in this town the way I used to," he replied.

"I can't even imagine how bizarre it would feel to visit my hometown now after all these years," I agreed, shaking my head. "I wonder if people would even recognize me."

Marshall smiled. "You're famous, Jesse. I'm sure they'd recognize you."

Blushing, I conceded the point. "I guess you got me there," I admitted with a soft chuckle.

Suddenly, Marshall pointed at something up ahead, his eyes bright and shining. "Look! Holy shit. The rumors are true," he said with more enthusiasm than I was used to from him.

I turned sideways in my seat, careful not to rock the canoe too hard, and laid eyes on the mythical-but-actually-real tiny island. I grinned from ear to ear, amazed. "My god. It's real. Should we go explore it?" I piped up.

"Hell yeah, we should," Marshall laughed. "Let's go!"

We paddled with renewed excitement, and I didn't even mind the ache in my biceps as we floated up to the small, densely vegetated island. Marshall used the rope to tether the canoe to a large boulder on the shore, and we hopped out, taking the lunch cooler with us. We spent the next hour or so just traipsing around on the island, which was packed with all kinds of small trees, bushes, and vibrantly colored wildflowers. I could definitely understand how this would seem like a mystical island to a bunch of small-town kids, and I even felt a bit like a kid myself as we explored. Finally, we found a smooth clearing where we sat down and devoured our lunch, having worked up an appetite between paddling and adventuring around. As we ate, we continued to chat about our pasts, our childhoods, the way things used to be. It was odd finding out that we had more in common than I would have expected, and I found myself hanging on Marshall's every word.

After lunch, we piled back into the canoe and went paddling around the lake some more, just working out our arms and enjoying the gorgeous weather. Once we had gotten our fill and the sun was starting to slip down toward the horizon indicating midafternoon, we diligently paddled back to the dock and tied up again. My whole body ached as we climbed out of the canoe and made our way back up to the lake house, but I couldn't stop smiling. We rinsed off in the shower and headed into the kitchen to have a beer and cook a healthy dinner together. We listened to old fifties records on the vintage record player while we chopped, sautéed, and plated up our dinner side by side. As we sat at the table eating, watching the sun set over the calm lake, Marshall broached another topic he seemed slightly edgy about.

"So, there's something I wanted to float by you," he began.

"Go on," I said, shoving a bite of delicious veggies into my mouth.

"Some of the guys I know locally are throwing a barbecue this weekend, and I was wondering if you'd like to go with me," he said.

I was surprised. "Really? I mean, that sounds amazing, but I don't know if a barbecue will be especially merciful on my diet right now," I said with a laugh.

Marshall grinned, his whole face lighting up. "Don't worry about that. Normally, around here, you'd have that right. But these guys are all really health-conscious themselves. There will be plenty of healthy food at this barbecue."

"Oh! Well, in that case..." I said, smiling. "Who all will be there?"

Marshall shifted uncomfortably in his seat, a subtle movement some might not notice, but I was highly tuned in to everything he said and did. He seemed uneasy when he explained, "My buddy Mason invited me. It'll be a bunch of guys I know from back in the day. All great people. Mason's been inviting me to all kinds of get-togethers. I just usually don't go," he admitted.

I frowned slightly. "Why not?"

"Just busy, I guess," he answered hastily. "Anyway, it should be a good time. Even with the healthy food."

I decided to let my query go for now, even though I longed to know more. We'd had such a wonderful day, I didn't want to do anything to spoil it. So instead I simply nodded and replied brightly, "Sounds good to me. I'm game!"

MARSHALL

NANCY SULLIVAN'S BARBECUE WAS TAKING PLACE ON A DAY WHERE JUST enough lazy clouds were providing some much-needed shade on an otherwise hot and sunny day. I would have expected nothing less. Sometimes I could have sworn the woman was a witch, but I meant that in the best possible way.

This time, I managed to convince Jesse to let me drive him since this was the definition of a personal event. A long stretch of curving road brought us around the bend of a quiet neighborhood, and we saw the line of cars parked on the side of the road outside the over-flowing driveway before we saw the property itself. When we did finally see the house and everyone milling around outside, I was glad I brought Jesse.

These people knew me, but few would say they knew me well, and none were as close as Jesse had become in a very short amount of time. I didn't mind that, generally, but I couldn't deny that it felt a lot better having him at my side.

The Sullivan house had recently had some major renovations done. And once she had her chance to get her dream house, Miss Nancy cut no corners. The large Victorian-style southern home sported incredible bay windows, a wraparound porch littered with a number of rocking chairs and outdoor coffee tables, a pond with a small bridge stretching over it, and what looked like a lovely raised bed garden that was starting to show some green in the backyard that we saw for just a moment as we rounded the bend. And of course, it was all filled out by at least two dozen people, all of them moving around the property and chatting with each other good-naturedly. Most had cups or glasses in hand, and I didn't have to be up close to know most of them contained sweet tea.

"I think someone took a picture of this house to advertise the town when I was looking into it," Jesse said, a broad smile spreading across his face. "I honestly wasn't sure if it was real; it looked so good it could have been staged."

"That's Miss Nancy," I said, shaking my head.

Not even I had been immune to her hospitality.

"You know her?" Jesse asked. "I mean, I guess it would be odd for us to be here if you didn't."

"Not all that odd," I said. "I'd be only half surprised if an invitation to this had turned up at your place, even if we'd never met. Bear traps and trip wires won't stop Miss Nancy if she wants to give you a warm welcome."

"I know exactly what you mean, so maybe I'm not that far from home after all," Jesse said.

"When I was a teenager, my mom had me pick up some groceries for her one week when we heard she was sick," I explained. "When I moved back to Winchester, she had three homemade pies waiting for me at my mom's place as a welcome home. I have no idea how she even found out I was coming back."

My witch theory had *some* basis, after all. Maybe psychic.

After we parked and got out, Jesse came around the front of the car, and I couldn't stop myself from taking a long look up and down his body. Jesse was wearing a blue-and-white-striped T-shirt that had its short sleeves cuffed at the biceps, and the whole piece of fabric showed that his torso was subtly just a bit trimmer than I remembered it at that first breakfast encounter. Two weeks could fly by in no time. Lower down, Jesse sported khaki shorts that did his thighs and butt a world of favors, and I had a hard time tearing my eyes away from them.

It was a welcome distraction from everything else that had my heart pounding. I did not typically make appearances at social events like this. I got invited all the time, but I usually had to be in a damn good mood to actually go to one of these things. It wasn't that I was afraid of anyone, I just liked to keep to myself. The idea of going with Jesse had seemed better, somehow, even though I couldn't place why exactly. I was attracted to him, so there was that, but I felt more *prepared* going in with him.

"What?" he asked when he caught me staring. "I'm not overdressed, am I? I don't have as many sleeveless shirts as you," he teased, grinning at my gray tank top.

"No," I grunted, "I just like your butt."

The blunt compliment took him off guard, like I hoped it would, and he turned his face away to half hide his grin.

"Speaking of…" he said, giving me a thoughtful look. "How should we… should it even come up that we're…?"

He was gesturing between us subtly, and I understood what he was asking. Frankly, I hadn't given much thought to what to call whatever we had going on romantically, and it was a relief that it seemed like Jesse hadn't, either. I nodded to show I caught his drift, and I thought for a moment.

"As much as I'd like showing you off," I said at last, "I don't see much good coming out of announcing anything. They'll probably figure it out on their own, and unless you want me to, I won't hide anything, either. That's just for your safety, though. *You* feel free to tell as much as you feel good telling," I added with a gruff smile.

That last bit was a rule that had gotten me through a lot in Winchester.

"Sounds perfect," Jesse said, beaming.

"Word of warning," I added as we started making our way across the yard toward the grills, "avoid the sweet tea."

"Oh," Jesse said, eyes widening. "So it's *that* kind of sweet tea?"

I nodded solemnly, and Jesse understood. Any further south than maybe Virginia, and there was a solid chance that the homemade sweet tea you drank was at least a third pure sugar. Further into the Carolinas, that figure was probably more like half.

Unsweetened tea had been nothing but "the diet choice" until about a decade ago. Fortunately for Jesse (unfortunately for his dentist, maybe), that was no longer the case. The sweet stuff was way too sweet for my tastes, anyway.

As soon as we entered the yard, I nodded for Jesse to follow close by me, and I led him to Miss Nancy, who looked like she was hovering around the grills. If I didn't say hello to her first, I'd be remiss. When we approached, she was standing with her hands on her hips next to another familiar face.

"Now Carter, tell me again what these things are made of?" she asked, looking suspiciously at the patties on the grill in front of him.

"These are black bean burgers," he explained, pointing out the darker patties on the grill before him. "Made 'em myself. They're really simple. Black beans, garlic and onion powder, smoked paprika, cumin, bread crumbs, and an egg."

"No meat in that at all, hm?" she asked, narrowing her eyes suspiciously as her nose twitched, and Carter laughed.

"No ma'am," he confirmed, "unless you count the egg."

"Now how on earth would someone count an egg as meat?" she said, genuinely surprised.

"Think that's called being a vegan, Miss Nancy," Carter answered through a grin.

"And that's... *different* from being vegetarian?" she asked cautiously, and I had to give her credit. She seemed like she was earnestly trying to get the terms down right.

"Vegan means no animal products at all," Carter explained, "like the franks I've got over here."

"And what's in those?" she asked suspiciously, sweeping around to Carter's side and picking up some tongs to flip the franks for him. "They don't split quite the same, but they smell all right," she admitted.

Getting traditional southerners to sink their teeth into vegetarian or vegan food seemed to be quickly becoming Carter's favorite pastime, and I had to admit, it looked like a fun challenge.

"All kinds of stuff," Carter said, "but mostly grains and veggies. Store-bought kinds can be heavy on oils, so I try to go all natural. If you've ever had a good sausage British-style, it's a little closer to that. Here, this one's done. Try half."

He lifted one off the grill and onto a plate, and Miss Nancy cut off a piece to chew on judiciously. As she did, she noticed our approach, and her face lit up. She quickly hurried up her chewing, and Carter gave me a friendly nod before doing the same to Jesse.

"Look who made it!" Miss Nancy finally said once she'd swallowed, and she beckoned me to bend over so she could give me a hug. "So good to see you again, sugar! Carter was just showing me some of what the boys are calling sawdust, but I've gotta say, it's not half bad!"

"High praise," I said over Miss Nancy's shoulder to Carter as I hugged her, and Carter chuckled.

"And who's this handsome gentleman?" Miss Nancy asked, looking at Jesse with stars in her eyes.

As if she didn't know exactly who Jesse Blackwood was. But that was exactly the kind of greeting I knew Jesse had been hoping for, and he looked delighted.

"Miss Nancy," I said, "meet Jesse Blackwood. You might have heard of him."

"Well, I sure reckon I have!" she said, laughing and hugging Jesse warmly. "Sweetheart, you're gonna have to forgive me if I slip up and call you Adrian at some point today."

"That's no problem at all, Miss Nancy. It's a pleasure to meet you," Jesse said, hugging her back.

"And this is Carter Foster, the contractor who did this house justice," I added, nodding to Carter, who shook Jesse's hand next.

"Nice to have you in town, Mr. Blackwood," Carter said politely.

"Just Jesse, please," Jesse waved off, smiling. "I swear I'm not crashing the party."

"He's my plus one," I said, feeling like that was a better explanation than outright saying I was his bodyguard.

Besides, if some of the other local guys overheard that, I wouldn't put it past them to take it as a challenge to try and make off with Jesse under my nose. As much as I would love to see one of them try, I didn't think that would be the best reintroduction to small-town life for Jesse.

"We're in South Carolina, honey. You can have as many pluses as you want to bring," Miss Nancy said with a wink.

"And I have to say," Jesse added, moving over to the grill with me, "I'd never thought I'd see the day that this much meatless food is on the grill. Even back in Knoxville, vegetarian places are only just starting to catch on."

"Funny story about that," Carter said brightly. "This isn't even the food that collects dust—there's more than enough to go around, but you'll be one of at least two of us going vegetarian today."

As if on cue, Mark Sullivan broke away from his conversation with a couple of other guests and approached the other side of the grills with a broad smile on his face at the sight of all of us. Carter leaned around the grill to peck Mark on the cheek, and Jesse's eyebrows went up.

He looked from me to them with a questioning look on his face, and when I nodded, his expression lit up.

"Was just talking about you," Carter said to Mark in a flirty tone. "Well, more about the food."

"Hey, I go hand in hand with good food, so no complaints there," Mark said, laughing.

I'd seen Mark around town plenty of times since his return to Winchester. Like me, he had moved away from Winchester for a while and worked remotely, but when he'd come back, he'd felt the need to start losing some weight and getting in shape. He had met Carter, who seemed to have an endless supply of healthy, home-grown food to help that process along, and I had to admit, it had been incredible to watch Mark's changes over time.

His eyes looked brighter, he never had circles under them, he was trim, and overall, he just seemed happier and more energetic. I remembered him as a shy guy back in high school, but now, he was a new man. And part of me hoped that bringing Jesse into company like this would make him feel even more at home by meeting him halfway.

"Jesse, Mark here is Miss Nancy's grandson and my boyfriend," Carter explained as Mark shook Jesse's hand. "He's who you can thank for having something healthy on the menu."

"Hey, Tyler and Mason are doing a pretty good job of helping us eat through all this, too," Mark noted. "I think Mason's going carnivore today, but Tyler keeps looking over here with that look in his eye."

"He's not the only one, just saying," Carter agreed with a soft laugh, and a glance around the barbecue proved him right.

The guys in attendance today were sometimes rough around the edges, but when all was said and done, they were just good country boys who liked to get rowdy sometimes. Most of them were hovering around the grills that were full of sizzling meat, and stacks of biscuits were piled high on the tables nearby with more than one container brimming with homemade sausage gravy that did not skimp on the sausage.

"Nice to meet you," Jesse said to Mark with a firm shake before addressing both of the Sullivans. "You two have a lovely family home. I can't get over how beautiful this place looks."

"All the better for these little get-togethers," Miss Nancy said. "Speaking of, Marshall, where's your mama today?"

"She's spending the day with a friend today, Miss Nancy," I answered, ignoring Jesse's curious glance my direction.

"Hey Jesse," Mark said, "if you're eating at our table today, you'll probably want to know where the drinks that aren't mostly sugar are."

"Uh, sure!" Jesse said after giving me a questioning glance. "I think I'll survive five minutes without you, don't you think?"

"Yeah, we're all right here," I said confidently, giving him a nod.

Jesse didn't know it, but I had taken a few extra steps to make sure this afternoon went smoothly. When I'd let the Sullivans know I'd be coming, I'd given them a heads-up about Jesse to ask them to be chill and keep an eye out for uninvited guests. Miss Nancy herself had assured me over text that she'd make sure *that* wasn't a problem, so Jesse could wander around and enjoy himself.

As he and Mark walked off with Miss Nancy—who decided now was a good time to advocate for the beauty of old-fashioned sweet tea —and I chuckled as I saw them get almost immediately intercepted by a group of locals who wanted to talk to Mark. Jesse looked comically out of place around this crowd, but the smile on his face and spark in his eyes told me I had done right by bringing him here.

"Hey," Carter said, snapping me out of my trance staring after Jesse. "So, how's that going, man? he asked with a nod toward Jesse.

"What, the job?" I said, crossing my arms. "Can't complain. Good pay, nice house."

"Well, sure, that's good too," he said with a meaningful smile.

I furrowed my brow.

"Think I might be missing something," I grunted.

"All I'm saying is, it's been a while since I've seen you smiling," Carter pointed out as he flipped the burgers one by one. "I don't mean to pry or anything, though."

It dawned on me what he was talking about, and I had to chuckle at myself and rub the back of my neck.

"That obvious, huh?" I asked.

"Nah," he assured me, "I just happened to see how you two were looking at each other when you got out of your truck. That, and you've got the same cologne on yourselves."

Ah, shit, I was wondering if anyone would notice. I never liked advertising my private life to the world, although Jesse was making it extremely tempting to break that habit.

"Don't worry. I won't say anything," Carter said.

"I don't mind," I said honestly. "Well, I wouldn't, but he has a few...security concerns, which you know about. I'd hate for rumors to get out that Jesse Blackwood is out here to be a playboy or something."

"Hey, no explanation needed," Carter said, beaming. "I was just surprised. I don't think I remember you seeing anyone but ladies back in the day."

"I'm as surprised as you," I admitted, a little embarrassed at myself, and I hesitated before saying anything further. "But... I was actually wondering if you'd mind sending me some of the recipes you used for all this," I said with a gesture around to all the food Carter was cooking. "Jesse's trying to get a little healthier while he's here."

"I'll do more than that, I'll give you free rein to take whatever you want from my garden," Carter said cheerfully. "I've got more than enough to go around. I swear the plants pick up on my good mood."

"Business booming that much for you?" I asked, smiling.

"Not just that," Carter said, blushing faintly and glancing over at Mark to make sure they were out of earshot before leaning in and whispering, "I got a ring for Mark."

My eyebrows shot up.

"Goddamn, congratulations!" I said, shaking Carter's hand and patting him on the shoulder. "Mark's a lucky man. It's been, uh, encouraging to see you two getting together."

Carter caught my drift, and he laughed softly.

"Hey, I know it can be wild to change so much about what you think you know about yourself," he said.

"It's kind of a rush, isn't it?" I said, feeling my heart pounding harder at the thought of what I felt with Jesse. "World of new feelings."

"In more ways than one," Carter agreed with a broad grin. "Ain't it the truth? But yeah, I didn't know what to make of it at first. I mean, I fell head over heels for Mark pretty quick, and I didn't feel a scrap of doubt about that."

I hadn't either.

"I kept expecting this big identity crisis or something, but I found that just leaning into it was... good," he said with an expression that spoke volumes. "Very, very good."

"So, keep doing what I'm doing," I said, rolling my shoulders back and nodding. "I can do that."

Carter looked at me thoughtfully for a moment before saying, "You're putting some thought into this, aren't you?"

Some color came to my cheeks, and before I could reply, I heard the sound of footsteps running our way. I turned to see Tyler approaching us with a football in his hands, and he let me see him drawing it back before tossing it to me. I caught it without having to move my feet, and I saw Mason approaching behind him.

"Hey Marshall!" Tyler greeted us as he trotted up. "You and Carter hurry up and get that food done. I want to get a pickup game going! Y'all in?"

Carter and I exchanged a glance before I looked over to the loose group of a dozen or so men who were gathering in the open lot next to the house. I cast a glance over at Jesse, who was on the porch with Mark and seemed to be telling a hilarious story to him, Miss Nancy, and a couple of women I vaguely remembered as being coworkers of Mason's from the gym who stopped in at The Chisel for a drink now and then. In short, he was well taken care of.

A game of football was a hard offer to turn down. I might have had a reputation around town that made some people uneasy, but these guys had made me feel welcome as a team member. That was something I could appreciate in spades, and I knew how to throw my weight around in a game.

I looked back to Tyler, and a wolfish grin spread across my face.

JESSE

My cheeks were starting to ache from smiling so much as I sat at one of the picnic tables arranged throughout Nancy Sullivan's front yard. It was a gorgeous, glorious sunny day, the kind I was accustomed to seeing back home in Los Angeles. Pure sunshine and blue skies as far as the eye could see in every direction, every now and then patterned with perfect, fluffy white clouds. If someone had presented to me a painting of the skies as they looked right now, I might have called it unrealistic. But here it all seemed so natural, much like the way it felt sitting here watching the guys play a pickup game of football. Admittedly, I had never known much about the game myself. Back in my school days, I had definitely hung around more with the theater and arts kids than the jocks. It wasn't so much that I'd disliked sports, more like I had stronger interests elsewhere. In the art department there had been a couple of kids who played soccer and volleyball who I'd considered friends. As a rule, though, for whatever arbitrary teenage reasoning, the football jocks and the theater kids had formed two totally separate groups. It hadn't even been a Venn Diagram. Just two circles, never touching for a single second. However, I had attended football games as a social event, especially in my senior year when I'd suddenly developed a brief surge of school pride and sentimentality. I'd never once understood the rules of the game or why it unfolded the way it did, but the contagious excitement of the crowds, the swell of music from the marching band pit, and the chanting, grinning cheer squad had made it all a uniquely immersive experience, despite how little I'd comprehended what was actually going on.

I felt pretty much the same way now, watching the guys throw the football up and down the imaginary field, shouting directions and commands to one another that sounded barely coherent to me but which probably made perfect sense to the players. It was the sensation that I was peeking through a window into a world that had little to do with me or my life, and I was somewhat fascinated by it. All the guys here seemed to be in great shape, with taut muscles and trim figures. On top of being handsome, they were all so down-to-earth and friendly, the very definition of southern hospitality at its absolute best. But for my eyes, there was only one hot body I couldn't tear my gaze away from, no matter how hard I tried.

Marshall. He was sprinting back and forth, those thick calf muscles bulging impressively as he switched direction and bolted the other way, twisting his body around to deftly catch the football as it sailed through the air to him. There was a brightness, almost a sparkle to his eyes as he enjoyed a little healthy competition, and it was truly entrancing to see him in action. After all, I had already known that Marshall was tough and strong. That was apparent just at first glance. But here, watching the game, I could see now that there was more to it than raw, blind strength and power. He knew exactly how to harness and channel that strength, and he was far more nimble and adept than one might think, judging by his bulky frame. He was a big guy—there was no doubt about that. But he wasn't just a brick wall of brute strength. He could dart left and right, dive for the ball, leap through the air, and tuck and roll along the grass with all the careful precision and lightness of a ballerina. It was impressive. I could see why the other guys had been so eager to get him on their respective teams. There were a lot of talented, highly athletic guys dashing around in the yard, but in my (possibly slightly biased) opinion, Marshall was the stand-out star of the game. Just watching the way his clothes clung to and accentuated every sharp line and curve of his powerful frame was enough to make my mouth water for more than just the delicious food on my plate. I could just imagine the way he would smell, all musky and grassy as we rode back to the lake house together. My heart skipped a beat at the prospect of hopping into the shower with him, watching those huge muscles ripple and tense as he lathered up and washed off all that sweat and grime. I wondered how he would feel about letting me join in. I would love the opportunity to massage hot, soapy water over his broad back, down his thick biceps, sliding down to that perfectly taut, round ass.

Damn. I was getting turned on just thinking about it.

But I was quickly shaken from my dirty thoughts by the sudden appearance of Miss Nancy, walking over to my table with a glass of sweet tea in her hand and a big, friendly smile on her face. She looked every bit the part of an ideal grandmother. I knew well enough from my years in Hollywood that if a director put out a casting call for a woman to play somebody's kindhearted, gentle grandmother, Miss Nancy would win the role every time without fail. I could definitely see why the guys around here flocked to her. She seemed to really care for them all, taking them under her wing like a mama duck. I hoped I could make a good impression on her, especially outside of just being a familiar face due to *Bannister Heights*. She had laughed at the dumb joke I'd made earlier, so it looked like we were off to a pretty positive start. Still, I wanted to keep up that momentum. Even though she wasn't Marshall's grandmother, of course, I still felt a powerful need to bond with her. I could tell he really respected Miss Nancy, and that meant something coming from a tough guy like him. If there was one thing my years of dating had taught me, it was that men like Marshall were not usually quick to trust others, so anyone he cared that much about had to be one hell of a fantastic human being. So I gladly scooted over to make room for the sweet, older lady.

"Why, thank you, sweetheart," she said warmly. "Best seat in the house, eh?"

She gestured vaguely toward the guys playing football, waggling her brows so that I laughed out loud. I nodded, grinning at her.

"You got that right, ma'am," I replied.

"Ma'am? My goodness! I didn't know they were teaching manners like that all the way out in balmy California!" she gushed, laying a delicate hand on my arm for a moment.

"Well, maybe it's because I'm not originally from L.A.," I confessed.

"Oh, that's right! You mentioned being from Knoxville, didn't you?" she asked, sounding genuinely interested as she peered at me over the brim of her teacup.

"Yes. Tennessee born and raised," I commented. "It hasn't been my home for a long time, but it's where I'm from."

"Knoxville's a fine city. A little too busy for me these days, but the food there is just to die for, isn't it?" she remarked.

I had to smile. "You got that right. The way I used to eat growing up, I'm amazed I was ever able to fit the clothes my mom picked out for me. All that gravy and butter and cream," I sighed nostalgically.

"Mhmm!" she agreed enthusiastically. "That's all the good stuff! I bet y'all don't eat a lot of gravy in Los Angeles, do you?"

I shook my head, laughing. "No, ma'am. It's all avocados and cucumbers out there," I told her. "But if you're ever in L.A., I can show you the good restaurants. There are a few good ones out there, believe it or not."

"Oh, I believe you, honey! A nice boy from Tennessee? No doubt in my mind, I know you know good food," she remarked with a wink.

"Now, I will say it's a little easier to stick to a diet back home. Everything here is so delicious I wish I could just eat everything," I lamented.

"I bet your agent makes you hit the gym every day, doesn't he? Oh, I've heard such crazy things about what actors such as yourself have to go through for a role," Miss Nancy said.

Coming from just about anyone else, I might have assumed she was being facetious, maybe even sarcastic. But I could tell right away from the moment I met her that Miss Nancy didn't have a cruel bone in her body. She was nothing but sincere.

"My guy is pretty laid back, actually, as far as Hollywood agents go," I replied. "As long as I know my lines, show up on time for hair and makeup, and don't cause any big tabloid scandals, he's happy."

"Oh, that's nice to hear. Movies always make them seem so shallow. But I guess that's just movie magic like anything else," she mused. "I have to ask: what's it really like being on set for *Bannister Heights*? I hope you don't mind me being nosy. It's just that we don't get an awful lot of famous actors here in little Winchester."s

"I don't mind at all," I said with a smile. "It's a great time. Long hours, lots of downtime just waiting for the next scene, but I love it. I've wanted to be an actor ever since I was a little boy, so it's a dream come true."

Miss Nancy looked so pleased with my answer I thought I saw what looked like the faintest shimmer of happy tears in her eyes. She leaned into me and said, "My goodness. That's just lovely. Good on you, Jesse!"

Just then, one of the guys who had been poking fun at the vegetarian food on offer earlier came sauntering past with a full plate, stacked high with black bean burger patties. When he saw that we were looking at him, his face flushed and he gave us a shrug and a sheepish grin.

"I might have spoken a little too soon about the bean patties. They're pretty damn good, actually. I'm havin' to eat my words, but at least it tastes great," he said, chuckling.

"Never too late to find somethin' new you like," Miss Nancy said sagely.

"Ain't that the truth," he said, giving me a pointed look before flitting his eyes over to Marshall, who was in the middle of a spectacular dive for the football.

It took me no time at all to figure out what he was implying, but judging by the smile on his face, he meant no harm. In fact, that seemed to be the case with everybody here. Even though I had worried at first that I might face some scrutiny or even outright pushback for being an openly gay, well-known actor coming to a small town in the South. But so far, I had met only the nicest, most well-intentioned people here. The more time I spent in Winchester, the more I wanted to stay here longer. It had taken me such a short time to start really feeling comfortable in this wonderful little town, defying even my loftiest hopes.

Of course, getting to spend most of my time with Marshall sure didn't hurt, either.

I could totally see how a guy like him could hail from a place like this. Winchester was accepting. It was thriving. And it was nourishing. It was the kind of town where people genuinely seemed to not only accept one another but actually get along, too. Everybody was eager to help out and lend a hand. Even just the straightforward, no-nonsense manner in which Marshall had brought over his exercise equipment for me to use without my asking seemed indicative of the way he was raised. And coming from Los Angeles, where friends could be fickle at best and downright duplicitous at worst, I was impressed. I felt pretty damn good about my decision to fly out here for my sabbatical. In fact, I was so pleased that I was beginning to muse about the idea of returning here on a yearly basis, maybe keeping a house on Lake Wren on retainer for visits. Or hell, I could even swing buying one outright so that I'd always have a place to call my own here in town.

And then I could spend more time with Marshall.

Watching him run up and down the makeshift football field was entertainment enough to last me a long while. He was usually so adept at hiding his emotions, good or bad, but I could tell he was truly enjoying himself out there, smiling and laughing, high-fiving his teammates and opponents alike. It was nice to see him come out of his shell for once. I wondered why he didn't do things like this more often.

"Miss Nancy," I began with a little caution, "how well do you know Marshall?"

She sighed wistfully. "I've known that boy since he was a little sprout. Well, not that he was ever what you could call 'little' to be honest," she said, smiling affectionately.

"Has he always been so... reluctant to put himself out there? He mentioned to me that he gets invitations to these events a lot but that he doesn't often attend. I wondered if you might be able to tell me why," I said softly.

"He's always been a little quiet, but I think things really got out of hand for him when he moved off to Atlanta to work for his uncle," she said, shaking her head. "I don't like to speak ill of people behind their backs, but I have to admit I've never really been a big fan of his uncle."

"Oh? Why's that?" I asked.

She pursed her lips for a moment as though weighing her words. Then she said in a lower voice, "Well, you know, he used to run with a kind of rowdy group back in the day. I always suspected he was up to somethin' bad. Marshall could've done just fine for himself here in town, but he wanted to branch out and see the world, so he followed his uncle to Atlanta. He was gone for a while. Ten years, in fact. And then, two years ago, he came home. Now, I don't put much stock in hearsay, but there have been rumors that his uncle's company got tangled up in some shady business. I don't know what exactly that would entail, especially in a town as small and insular as Winchester. But that's what I've heard, you know, through the grapevine."

"Wow," I murmured, watching Marshall artfully tuck and roll with the football. "I had no idea about any of that."

"Now, don't you let any of that color your ideas about Marshall himself. He's a good boy, no matter what kind of shenanigans his rotten uncle may be into. Trust me—that Marshall's got a steady head on his shoulders and goodness in his heart. No doubt about that. People talk. There's no way 'round that. But any rumors about Marshall should be put to rest. He doesn't have a bad bone in his body," she said emphatically.

"That I can definitely believe," I replied warmly.

* * *

THE NEXT MORNING, Marshall admitted he was feeling a little sore from the game. And from what I had witnessed of the football match, I could definitely understand why. Not even a seasoned athlete at any age could have moved like he did without feeling some residual soreness. But I was fine with it, as it gave me a fantastic chance to spoil him a little as thanks for all the hard work he'd been putting in for me. So when I woke up before the alarm, just in time to turn it off so it wouldn't wake him, I sneaked out of the bedroom and downstairs to cook him up a healthy breakfast of scrambled egg whites with turkey bacon, spinach, Roma tomatoes, and mushrooms and a side of wheat toast. I brought it to him in bed along with a cup of black coffee, and the look on his face when he woke up to the smell of delicious breakfast was more than enough to make my day.

We sat in bed together, just chatting and enjoying the bright morning sunshine streaming in through the window. We talked about how much fun we'd both had at the barbecue at the Sullivan house, already reminiscing about the amazing food and great company. The two of us took our time with breakfast, feeling in no big rush to get the day going, but when we finished eating, Marshall announced that he was going to take a long, hot shower to ease his tired muscles. I kissed him on the cheek, and he went off to wash up while I stayed in bed with my laptop and a steaming cup of coffee.

Even though we had spent a lovely morning together so far, I still couldn't quite shake the conversation I'd shared with Miss Nancy regarding Marshall's background. There was a persistent voice in the back of my head urging me to look into it, even though I trusted Marshall completely. Still, I couldn't keep myself from snooping a little while he was in the shower. I searched for the company Marshall once worked for, and when I found solid proof that he had, indeed, worked for his uncle's company, my heart started racing. I kept pushing the issue and discovered that one of his uncle's business ventures was a nightclub that had gotten closed down due to an ongoing tax fraud investigation. From there, I stumbled into another, even more unnerving discovery: that there were even allegations of mafia connections involved with the failed nightclub. Of course, these allegations were thus far unproven, but it was still disturbing to find out there were even whispers of such a scandal. Just as I was starting to dig too deep, I realized that the sound of the shower running had stopped. I closed out of my multiple search tabs just as Marshall came sauntering out of the bathroom, a puff of steam escaping along with him. I turned and gave him a winning smile, doing a double take when I set eyes on his glorious body, naked except for a small towel wrapped around his waist. I set my laptop aside as well as my concerns, at least for the time being.

After all, how could I get caught up in the what-ifs when he was standing right there in front of me, gorgeous and flawless as always?

MARSHALL

Two full days after Jesse and I went to the barbecue, I was watching him put the subtle changes I'd noticed in his body to real use.

His biceps glistened in the morning sunlight as I watched them work the oar in his hands stroke after stroke. He was sitting in the front of the canoe, while I was sitting in the back, enjoying the view of his muscles working together perfectly to steer our small vessel through the sweet-smelling waters. Jesse had improved, and it showed.

His oar dipped into the glassy water and glided through the stroke with power and grace before switching sides and doing the same on the other. I was almost hypnotized, not by the wood on water, but by the way his shoulders rippled each time he changed hands. His forearms were starting to show their strength each time he lowered the oar into the water and moved it.

From the back, I was giving the canoe the most speed, while Jesse handled steering, but even my workload felt lighter this morning.

"I'm surprised we don't see more people out here," Jesse remarked, speaking softly yet clearly enough that I could hear him easily over the stillness of the lake. "It's a perfect day for this."

"We're a ways away from the main spots people launch from," I said, not able to keep my voice as gentle but nonetheless lower. "Serious athletes might come and go earlier than we get up, but not many tourists."

Being able to say *we* got up together was always an oddly pleasant surprise whenever there was a reason for the words to roll off my tongue. It felt right. Jesse was the one who was taking some personal time, but I found myself feeling like I was on vacation while still handling security.

That might have even been part of what made me like this whole situation.

Setting up all these security cameras, watching over the property protectively, feeling like I was keeping Jesse safe, it all felt very domestic to me. Waking up to this man in bed next to me every morning had changed how I looked at the job, so much so that it was funny to think back to a couple of weeks ago when I'd thought of this as babysitting some spoiled celebrity. But now that Jesse was close to me like this, now that we shared dinners and could share each other's feelings and worries and be intimate, I didn't feel like I was bodyguarding a client anymore. I felt like I was caring for someone, caring in a better way than I'd thought possible.

Jesse looked over his shoulder and met my gaze, and he blinked at me a couple of times.

"Everything all right?" he asked.

"Hm? What do you mean?"

"You just had that thousand-yard look in your eye, like you were having flashbacks or something," he said, cracking a smile.

"Oh," I said, ignoring the faint tinge of color coming to my face. "Just watching your technique. You're getting good at this, you know."

"I have a good teacher," he fired back without missing a beat.

He was getting better at deflecting my compliments, too, which I couldn't help but find adorable. Those acting skills came in real handy now and then, I had to admit.

"How are you liking your results so far?" I asked.

"This feels a lot more natural," he admitted, and I was glad to hear him affirm his progress. "But before I say anything else, what do *you* think about my progress?" he asked with a playful undertone.

"I think I haven't been able to keep my hands off you from the start up through now, and that should tell you exactly what I think," I growled, and goose bumps pricked up on Jesse's neck.

The little things about Jesse like that gave me special satisfaction.

"Then you could say I'm pretty happy I came down here, yeah," he flirted back with that glint in his eye.

Getting that kind of reaction out of him made my heart flutter, and I wasn't the kind of guy who thought his heart would ever be doing something I could describe as fluttering. I wanted to keep making him blush like that, and I wanted to go places with him too, for that matter. I couldn't deny it. I was falling for him hard.

I had crushed on people plenty of times before in my thirty-two years of life, and it hadn't felt quite like this. Maybe it was the newness of everything, but something in me knew that wasn't a satisfying answer. All I knew was that I liked it. I liked *him*.

We reached our usual turning point and swung the canoe around to start paddling toward the lake house again without much else said. And each moment that passed in silence, I felt a twinge of guilt. I had been lying when I said nothing was on my mind, but it wasn't anything bad. On the contrary, it was a good thing, but one that I wasn't sure how to bring up smoothly.

When in doubt, though, there was always the usual, less-than-smooth approach.

"Do you like antiquing?" I asked out of the blue.

Jesse was so surprised he actually stopped paddling, paused, and looked back at me in bewilderment.

"Who are you, and what have you done with Marshall Hawkins?" he asked, and I shook my head with a single deep laugh.

"No, no, I'm serious. This isn't that serious, though. Well, it is, but –" I grunted in frustration, scratching my head while Jesse watched me with a mix of curiosity and amusement. "My point is, it's my mom's birthday tomorrow."

Jesse's eyes widened and sparkled before his smile did the same, and he resumed paddling as he spoke over his shoulder.

"Oh!" he said. "I had no idea—please, take the day off. I insist. Don't try to say otherwise. I'll be perfectly fine for one day. I don't think anyone's dared try to get through the perimeter, much less tried to snap a photo of me lately."

"I appreciate it, but that wasn't what I was going to ask," I said, smiling. "Look, no pressure if this isn't your kind of thing, but... I was planning on taking her to Mill's Brook tomorrow to do some shopping, and I wanted to see if you'd like to come."

Jesse paused for a beat to grin back at me.

"What?" I asked gruffly, raising an eyebrow.

"I'm sorry, but I feel like I keep seeing bits and pieces of this adorable secret life you lead with your mom, and of *course* I'd be honored to come with you two," he gushed, and my face burned, even though I was grinning.

I smirked and smacked the water gently with my paddle, splashing Jesse with a bit of water, and he splashed back, laughing.

"It's not a secret," I grumbled in protest. "I just don't advertise myself."

"I think it's sweet," Jesse said matter-of-factly.

"Well... thanks," I admitted on a more sincere note, still smiling. "Anyway, sounds good. I'll call her tonight and let her know. She watches the show, fair warning, but she's cool."

"I mean..." Jesse said in that voice that meant he had an idea. "I don't want a fan to think I hate my character or anything, so if it's her birthday, I could think of something she might like."

* * *

THE NEXT DAY, against all my better judgment, I was watching from the sidewalk as Jesse knocked on the door of my mother's little canary-yellow house on a corner of a cozy suburb of the town. And he was dressed as his character, Adrian Bannister.

Specifically, Jesse explained, he was dressed as Adrian Bannister from what was apparently a very iconic outfit from a couple of seasons ago, from a scene that won him an award. Jesse had described a vivid impression of it for me. It was the wedding ceremony at a beautiful chapel in the mountains, where a storm overhead was raging as Adrian's ex-lover, Beatrice, was walking down the aisle with his brother, Abel. Adrian's supposed private jet crash several episodes ago meant the season-long love triangle arc was finally coming to a close. Suddenly, a clap of thunder and the chapel doors swinging open announced the appearance of none other than Adrian, standing in the doorway drenched in rain in the signature black suit and red paisley tie.

Adrian swept Beatrice off her feet along with the audience, and the soap opera went on with renewed energy.

I had made Jesse promise to ditch the tie and jacket so that he wouldn't have a heat stroke in the hot summer sun later in the day, but he had insisted on this.

He leaned an arm on the doorpost dramatically as it opened, and as my mom appeared in the doorway, an overjoyed look crossed her face. I had to laugh as I watched Jesse bow his head politely while saying something—his opening lines in *Bannister Heights*, apparently—and my mom let out a cackle of amusement before meeting Jesse in her usual tight hug. That was my cue to approach, and she immediately bustled past Jesse to give me the same treatment. I was a little more used to it.

"Happy birthday, Mom," I said good-naturedly through a tight windpipe as she laughed, and I presented her with the small bouquet of flowers I had been holding behind my back.

"Oh my god, I just about had a heart attack, boy! I can*not* believe it," my mom gushed before kissing me on the cheek and turning to Jesse with a glowing smile, jabbing a thumb at me with a loving smile. "Did this troublemaker make you dress up like that just for me?"

"I swear he's innocent!" Jesse said with a big grin, slipping off the jacket and unbuttoning the sleeves. "This one was my idea. It's nice to meet you, Ms. Hawkins. Happy birthday."

"You boys are too much," she said, delighted. "Marshall warned me you were a sweetheart."

Mom was in her early fifties, but she had so much energy you'd think she was younger. She was a tall woman with a shorter haircut and favored jeans and T-shirts, and as a lifelong electrician, she had never had much use for a lot of deviation from that.

"I told you you'd be hot in that getup," I said to Jesse with a smug grin.

"Anything for the role," Jesse said with faux-drama as he took off the tie and rolled up his sleeves. "So, should we get on the road before anything else?"

"It's an hour's drive, so that sounds lovely," said Mom. "Let me just get these flowers in a vase, and we'll get on the road."

The drive to Mill's Brook was more or less one long, curving direct route down the highway, which gave us plenty of time to make proper introductions on the way over. Jesse got to go over the basics that he had given me about what brought him down to Winchester, while Mom got to rave about some of her favorite restaurants and cafés to hit up. Winchester was a small town, but we had our share of tourists, so we had a few more places like that than you might expect from a town of our size.

Jesse had insisted on letting Mom take the front seat, so he leaned between our seats while talking about life in L.A., which Mom had endless questions about. I couldn't help but smile. She had done the same thing to me when I moved to Atlanta. Big city life was something that fascinated my mother to no end, for some reason, but she'd never dream of actually moving to one. Jesse even brought up a little celebrity gossip unprompted.

Maybe he had taken enough of a break from being a celebrity that he didn't mind indulging a fan. Either way, it kept the conversation so snappy for the whole trip that it flew by in the blink of an eye.

Small town antique stores were an odd experience. Vintage was getting popular in more urban areas, but most of the 'serious' antique hunters didn't make it this far out into rural territory. That was why there was only one other car in the parking lot of the cute little store we pulled up to at last.

Inside, the smell of very old wood varnish and dust greeted me instantly, and I felt my sinuses protesting. The shop was much larger on the inside than the outside made it seem, and it was made of aisles upon aisles of shelves and displays of various kinds that seemed to stick to absolutely no kind of pattern. The place looked like the possessions of three generations had been shoved onto every open surface. There was a white-haired old couple behind the counter, one of whom was watching TV while the other played Sudoku and glanced up at us kindly.

In other words, it was a perfect antique store.

"Have you ever gone out for this kind of thing before?" I asked Jesse quietly as Mom wasted no time hurrying over to the books section.

"Heard of it, but it hasn't even crossed my mind, no," Jesse admitted, though he was grinning at the store around us. "I didn't think you would be the type either, honestly."

"I'm not," I said, "or at least I wasn't. I started coming out here with Mom when she asked, but it turns out you can find a lot of good sh-stuff here," I finished carefully.

Jesse stared at me for a second in confusion before a smile crept over his features. "Do you...not swear in front of your mother?"

I gave him a stony look in reply, and Jesse looked like his heart was melting. I gave him a gruff smile but rolled my eyes and walked down the aisle, carefully moving down a narrow row of china displays to see what Mom was suddenly interested in.

"Marshall, would you look at these cabinets?" she said, running her hand over the side of one of the faded mint green cabinets with chipping wood. "They're just like the ones we used to have when you were just a little slip of a thing!"

"Hard to imagine Marshall was ever little," Jesse teased, appearing behind me.

"Well, 'little' is relative," she said, opening one of the cabinet doors. "Remember those little plastic stoppers you used to be able to get for cabinets that were supposed to 'child proof' them?" Mom rolled her eyes with a smirk, and I knew where this was going. "Marshall found out that was where I kept the cereal, so one morning I hear this cracking of wood, and I run into the kitchen, scared to death... just to find him standing there with his cereal, happy as a clam, having just torn the door open and taken the stopper with it."

Jesse couldn't hold back a laugh, and even I had to chuckle. I remembered that day or at least that scene out of my childhood. I must have been about five.

"That was a good day," I decided aloud, then looked down at the cabinets, which had a reasonable price tag on them. "Don't suppose you need any new cabinets?"

"Well, I could always use more storage space, and now that I finally moved the fridge, I've got some extra room on that south wall," she remarked, stroking her chin.

"Why not these?" I suggested, patting the cabinets. "I could give 'em a fresh coat of paint and finish, make a project out of it."

"Oh, don't go doing all that," Mom tried to laugh off, but Jesse had my back.

"I actually didn't have time to get you a birthday present, Ms. Hawkins, so I think Marshall and I could go half and half on this one," Jesse said to me with a sly wink that made me grin.

"Well, if you're gonna insist," Mom said, and Jesse whistled innocently as he moved past us to investigate some old movie posters.

As soon as his back was turned, Mom looked back at me with a somehow knowing smile, and she nodded in Jesse's direction.

"I like this one," she whispered

"Yes ma'am," I said softly, looking after Jesse. "I do too."

AFTER DROPPING my mom off and waving to her as I pulled away, Jesse sat there with a broad smile on his face for almost a full thirty seconds as we drove out of the neighborhood before he finally couldn't resist looking over at me.

"What?" I said, laughing, feeling like we were back on the canoes again.

"Of all people who could have *that* adorable of a relationship-"

"Oh my god."

"With the *sweetest* mom."

"Jesse."

"Okay, I'm teasing, but in all seriousness," Jesse said as he leaned his seat back and looked at me admiringly, "not a lot of guys have that kind of relationship with their moms, here or in the city. It's really nice to see something like that. You're a good son, Marshall."

I felt my heart warm at those words, despite myself, and I allowed myself a smile. I would usually ignore compliments on my body or my skills at my job, but Mom was a different matter.

"She deserves the best," I said. "Not to get all sappy on you, but it was just me and Mom when I was growing up. Never had a dad in the picture, never gave him much thought. Mom was happy with it that way, and I was too. She's one of the best electricians in the whole county, if you ask me, so money was never really a problem for us, thanks to her hard work. So yeah, I love her, and I want to give her the best." I glanced over at Jesse with a modest smile. "Simple as that."

Jesse looked at me long and hard for a few moments. His face was smiling, but his eyes were narrowed as if he was trying to read something about me or figure me out.

"You know, I want to be surprised to hear all that, but I don't think I am," he said thoughtfully.

"Really?" I grunted. "I need to work harder, then."

"No, I mean it," he said, turning in his seat to face me better. "I don't think people give you enough credit, Marshall. You're not all that comes on the tin."

"Now I *know* I need to work harder at that," I said, chuckling.

"I don't know. I'm liking what I'm learning," he said, putting his arm on the center console.

Without even thinking about it, I reached over and clasped his hand in my bigger one, and I felt a fulfilling warmth in my chest.

We got inside, locked the door behind us, kicked off our shoes, and just like that, we had our privacy again. I never thought it would feel so good shutting the rest of the world out with just Jesse, but it felt like what true alone time should have felt like.

"What are you thinking for dinner?" Jesse asked as he headed for the kitchen, but before he could clear the living room, I followed him.

I grabbed him by the hips, spun him around, and pressed a kiss to his lips. He was surprised at first, but that quickly melted away. I put my hands on his hips and squeezed him, and I walked him backward to pin him against a wall and grind my hips back and forth, slowly.

"What was that for?" he asked when the kiss broke.

"My way of saying thank you," I growled.

"For going out with you today?" he asked, laughing lightly.

"More than that," I said, and I stood back to pick Jesse up before saying another word.

Holding him against me was easy, and he wrapped his legs around me as I held his ass and carried him up the stairs. I walked us all the way to the master bedroom, where I stepped inside and knelt on the bed before slowly letting Jesse down, never breaking eye contact.

"I didn't know what I was getting into with you," I admitted, "but you brought me out of my comfort zone. In more ways than one. I'm not used to that. And I'm not good with words. But I'm glad you did it. Doing this stuff with you feels…" I paused for a moment, struggling for the right words. "Better."

Jesse looked touched, and there was more than just lust in the gaze he met me with. He reached up to stroke the side of my face, and his thumb ran along my jawline, feeling its shape and definition.

"I like it better with you too, Marshall," he said softly, and I leaned down to press a deep, meaningful kiss to his mouth as our hearts pounded fiercely together, and my swelling cock pulsed against him.

JESSE

"How in the world did I manage to get so lucky?" I murmured against Marshall's soft, sensual lips.

I meant it. I could feel the power in his every touch, in the way he held me so firmly and yet almost gently at the same time. I was quickly learning that Marshall was a man of odd dichotomies. He was fierce and tough, with a scowl that could peel paint off a wall. And yet, he had the compassion and patience to genuinely enjoy a day out shopping in antique stores with his beloved mother. The way he had handled the ball, as well as the other players, in that pickup football game at the Sullivan barbecue was downright awe-inspiring, not to mention a little intimidating. But at the same time, he'd treated Miss Nancy like she was something precious, to be regarded with respect and reverence. He could pin me against a wall, flip me around, show me he was definitely the boss— but when he wanted to, he could be out and out romantic.

It seemed like there was no end to the surprises Marshall had to offer. Even though we spent damn near every moment together, I was constantly learning new, intriguing facets of his personality. I was fascinated with everything about him— his childhood, his adolescence, his family, his friends, even the little things like how he liked his eggs cooked (just cooked enough to be mostly solid, but not browned). Every day felt like I was adding another precious piece to the million-part jigsaw puzzle that represented who Marshall was on the inside. And it never got boring. Each and every waking moment spent in his company felt like a gift I would hold on to for the rest of my life, immortalized in memory. I had a feeling I could spend an eternity just watching him, following the curved lines and sharp cuts of his body as he moved through the world. I could get lost tracing the shape of his lips, the gentle bend of his nose, the quiet brilliance in his eyes.

When he looked at me, the world around us fell away. None of it mattered much when he was around, and yet, at the same time, everything mattered so much more. I found myself wanting to be better, to do better, just on the off chance he might notice. I wanted to make the world a better place. I wanted to become the man Marshall deserved, through and through. I was constantly seeking to impress him, but it wasn't the same way I felt the need to impress people back home in Los Angeles. It wasn't a desperate need to be admired. It wasn't a plea for more roles, bigger audiences, higher salaries, more prestigious awards. It was a simple drive to match him stroke for stroke, turn myself into the best version of Jesse Blackwood. The version who could stand side by side with the amazing Marshall Hawkins and keep up.

I didn't know if I could ever fully catch up to him. I had never met a person who was so quietly, subtly fantastic. There was no pretense with Marshall. He was a paragon of honesty, an ideal of straightforward truth. Even the little things he kept hidden for now, like whatever happened with his uncle's company, seemed trivial compared to all the good stuff.

And with Marshall, there was a hell of a lot of good stuff to speak of.

Right now, it was most notably his glorious, hard cock pressing tightly against my pelvis. I could feel every inch of his length sliding up and down, every other stroke brushing along my own quickly stiffening shaft, the two of us rutting together in perfect, seamless tandem. It was so easy with him, always. Everything felt so natural and good, like we had been cut from the same cloth to fit perfectly together. I knew, deep in the most logical part of my brain, that on paper we had almost nothing in common. Well, besides both being born and raised in the South. But I had changed so much since my Tennessee days. I had lived in Hollywood so long that sometimes the Knoxville version of myself seemed more like a distant cousin than my own image. And yet, despite how many differences I could tally up between us, it felt as though at the end of the day, we managed to end up in the same place. The same vibrations. The same desires. And to be wanted by a man like Marshall Hawkins? I couldn't imagine a more prestigious award than that.

"I could hardly resist you today," Marshall growled against the shell of my ear, sending delicious shivers down my spine.

I bucked my hips, grinding up into him, both of us moaning into each other's mouths in the low light of the bedroom. The sun was sinking to the horizon, and I knew if I could tear my eyes away from the incredible man on top of me for even a second, I would get to see the sky brilliantly streaked with pink and orange hues like a summertime sherbet. But I was totally enraptured with the man pinning me down, the one whose strong arms held me in a lover's embrace. I felt his breath hot on my neck and goose bumps prickled up along my arms and legs as he leaned in to gently bite my bottom lip. I groaned, involuntarily rocking my hips at the pleasantly sharp sensation.

And when he reached to pin both my wrists up above my head, I nearly lost my composure completely.

"You're sexy as hell, you know that, right?" I purred breathlessly.

"Well, it's easy to get into the mood when I spend all my time staring at your ass," he hissed back, dipping down to kiss deep, almost bruising marks along my collarbone. My chest was heaving, my heart racing a mile a minute. It was amazing to me how no matter how many times we did this together, it never failed to get me all riled up. Marshall just had that kind of effect on me. It was the closest thing to magic I could imagine in the real world.

"With your help, hopefully my ass is only going to get better and better," I tossed back, grinning.

"You've got to learn to just take a compliment and take credit once in a while, Jesse." He laughed gently. "If there's one thing I'm bound and determined to teach you, it's that."

"You're one to talk, but I'm open to whatever you have to teach me," I replied suggestively, hoping to make an impression with that one.

Marshall smirked at me, and I knew I'd struck just the right nerve.

"This—all of this," he growled, gesturing broadly to my clothes, "has to go."

He tugged at the bottom hem of my shirt, and I arched my back to let him pull it up over my head and arms, tossing it aside.

"Your turn," I said playfully, eyeing his shirt.

He gave me a grin and reared back on his knees, peeling off his shirt to reveal his incredible biceps, pectorals, and his taut, hard stomach. I couldn't help but lick my lips in anticipation, my eyes locked onto Marshall as he began unzipping his jeans. He slid off the bed to whip them off along with his boxers, and my mouth watered at the sight of his naked body. Marshall was built like a Greek statue, all sinew and perfectly sculpted muscle. Well, except for the fact that there was a pretty big difference between those classical statues and Marshall's body. His cock. It was massive, just about as intimidating to behold as the rest of him, but I wasn't one to shy away from a challenge, and this was one test I was happy to take again and again and again. I quickly whipped off my pants and boxers, kicking them off the end of the bed as Marshall came back over to straddle me. He grabbed my arms and pinned them up above my head again, groaning with pleasure as he rutted his cock along mine, the friction sending spirals of intense pleasure up through my body. I was fully under his spell, willing to give him whatever he wanted, whatever he needed. I was his for the taking, and instead of freaking me out, that knowledge only spurred me on to want him more.

"Sometimes, I can hardly believe you're real," I murmured as he reached over to the nightstand, pulling open the drawer. "It's like you stepped right out of my dreams."

"Right back at you," he rumbled.

The breath caught in my throat as I watched him take a condom from the nightstand and slowly, methodically roll it up over his thick cock, encasing the glimmering drop of precome beaded at the head. Then he took a small bottle of lubricant and squirted some over his fingers, his eyes locking with mine as he leaned over me. I felt his cock, slick in the condom, slide up against mine, the increased smoothness adding a new sensation to the mix. And when he groped my ass, moving his fingers closer and closer to my opening, I couldn't help but hold my breath again. As soon as his fingertips brushed over the tense, tight band of muscles there, I let it all out in a sharp gasp. The satisfied look on Marshall's handsome face only made me want him more. My cock throbbed and twitched as he slowly worked his fingers inside of me. I arched my back and rolled my eyes back, shutting them as I gave in to the waves of pleasure. I felt my body opening, blooming for him as he coaxed me into position. I bit my lip and cracked one eye open just in time to see his gaze flick up to mine.

"God, I want you so badly," he murmured gruffly, shaking his head.

"Then take me. I'm yours. Whenever, wherever," I replied in a whisper.

A flicker of a smile crossed his face, and then I felt the thick, engorged head of his cock press against my ass. I tensed up, my hands curling into fists above my head as he pushed inside inch by inch, filling me up with his massive cock. My eyelids fluttered, and I inhaled sharply, the mingled sensations of mild pain and incredible, mind-numbing pleasure flooding my body. Marshall groaned as he sheathed himself entirely inside me, the head of his shaft brushing against my prostate. He dipped down to kiss me, swallowing down the moan that fell from my lips. He reared back gradually, sliding almost all the way out before slamming back into me, hard. I gasped, and his arms fell around me, soothing me, brushing the stray strands of hair back from my temples. He kissed my lips, my cheeks, my forehead, his hands sliding up and down my body as he fucked me, both of us panting with bliss. When we moved together in flawless rhythm like this, it felt almost as though we were two parts of one well-oiled machine. Our bodies slid and stretched and pistoned alongside one another. We both cared so deeply about one another's pleasure, and it showed. Every stroke of his shaft inside me brought us closer and closer to the edge.

"Fuck, that's good," I mumbled.

"*You're* good," he hissed back.

His hand slid up my arms to grasp my curled fists, and then his other hand came up, too. He spread my hands apart and interlaced his fingers with mine as he picked up the pace, slipping in and out of my tight hole. We rocked together, groaning and gasping each other's names as the tension built up. I felt my chest growing tighter, matching the clench of Marshall's body over mine. He bit his lip, fucking me slowly but deeply, every stroke hitting that perfect, delicious spot inside me. My cock twitched and stiffened, my balls tightening. We drew nearer and nearer to that glorious edge. We danced closer, then away. Close, then away. Every time bringing us almost to the brink. Marshall gasped and rested his forehead against mine. His fingers tightened their grip on my hands and, with one more perfect stroke, we came together. I felt his cock throb and clench, filling the condom inside of me while I spurted hot, sticky come over my abdomen between us. We continued to hold each other, panting breathlessly together as we rode out the aftershocks of immense pleasure.

Finally, once we were totally spent, Marshall withdrew and slid off the bed. I watched him adoringly as he headed straight to the bathroom to get cleaned up, then abruptly turned back around to lean down and kiss me softly on the lips. I felt a tingling warmth shoot through my body at this gentle touch, and I couldn't help but feel like something serious had transpired between us. Something big. Something real.

He took my hand and pulled me up, gesturing for me to come with him.

"Come on. Let's get cleaned up before we start on dinner," he said, smiling.

I could hardly say no. I stood up and followed him into the en suite bathroom, grabbing my phone from the nightstand. I realized that even though I was on sabbatical and definitely more interested in Marshall than anything that could possibly be going on back in L.A., I still probably needed to keep abreast of things.

Just as Marshall was climbing into the steamy hot shower, my phone buzzed in my hand, indicating a new email. From behind the shower curtain, I heard Marshall say playfully, "Put the phone down and get in here."

"I'm coming," I said.

"I think you already did," he teased, making me roll my eyes even as I grinned.

"Ha-ha," I replied. "Hilarious."

"It's true. I mean, we both did," he added. I could almost hear the smirk in his tone.

"I'll be there in a sec. Let me just check this email," I murmured, scrolling through my phone. I opened the new email and read over it, my heart starting to race.

"What is it? Anything interesting?" Marshall asked over the rush of water.

"Uh, yes, actually. It's an invitation," I said.

"An invitation?" he repeated. "To what?"

"A party. A big party. A big, fancy party," I amended. "There's this guy—"

"A guy?" Marshall said. The slight concern in his voice made me smile.

"Yeah, but not that kind of guy," I said quickly. "He's an older actor, kind of a mentor of mine. He helped me kick off my career in Los Angeles years ago, and we've kept in touch ever since. Anyway, he's throwing a big bash this weekend, and I'm invited. Plus one."

"In Los Angeles?" Marshall asked.

"Yeah," I said. My heart was thumping like crazy, not knowing how he'd react.

"Sounds cool," he said. "You going to attend?"

"I don't know. I mean, I feel obligated to go because this guy's an old friend and a really good mentor. Plus, you know, half of the job of being an actor is just schmoozing with the right crowd. And trust me, this party will definitely have the right crowd," I said.

"All right. So, what's your hesitation?" Marshall remarked, poking his head out of the shower. I couldn't help but laugh at his wet, slicked-back hair. He raised an eyebrow. "You'd better get in here, Jesse. You're a mess."

I looked down at myself and realized he was right. I decided to shelve the phone for a moment and hopped into the shower with Marshall.

"My only worry is that I don't want to break my healthy streak by attending a Hollywood party. You would not believe the quality of food these parties have catered. It's unreal," I sighed.

"Well, I'd hate for you to miss out on a networking opportunity just because of a few extra calorie temptations," Marshall said thoughtfully. "So here's my offer: I'll go with you as your plus one. Not just as your bodyguard but... as a date. A date who will hold you accountable to your diet, if that's what you're so worried about."

I smiled, so overwhelmed with happiness that I couldn't help but lean in and kiss him on the lips. "Wow, that good, huh?" he murmured teasingly.

"Mhm," I said with a nod. "Marshall Hawkins in Los Angeles. What a treat."

"Don't get used to it," he warned, even though he was grinning from ear to ear.

"God, I can't wait to show you off," I said, and I meant every word.

MARSHALL

I NEVER THOUGHT I'D SEE L.A., MUCH LESS SEE IT FROM THIS VIEW. I was standing on the balcony of Jesse's apartment just a few days after he'd received his invitation, looking out over the glowing skyline of the city in dress pants and a tank top, leaning on the railing and staring down at the little dots of traffic below.

It had been about three weeks since I first met Jesse, and it had been three weeks that had careened through my life harder and faster than I could have possibly ever prepared for. Packing my bags and jetting off to L.A. was such a quick process that it reminded me of running security back in Atlanta. Jesse had been such a down-to-earth guy to get to know over the past few weeks that half the time I'd even forgotten he was an actor. The celebrity part wasn't as easy to forget, since I spent time each night going over the CCTV footage around the property and making sure we hadn't been intruded upon.

I was even keeping an eye on the place while traveling, which Jesse said really wasn't necessary, but I figured it would be worth the precaution.

Jesse's apartment was stunning. It wasn't overly luxurious, of course, but I would have expected nothing different from Jesse. That was just the kind of guy he was. Even so, this apartment was nicer than any I'd been in so far. The chocolate-brown wood floors stood out beautifully against the sleek, modern eggshell-white walls and slanted windows in the ceiling that drenched the floors in the orange sunlight of the late afternoon.

I could tell why Jesse had picked out the lake house in Winchester. The man loved his windows. Huge panels of square window patterns that gave the apartment almost the same vibe as an art gallery were in almost every room that didn't demand privacy.

Funny, despite being an actor on television, he didn't have one in his living room. A large and comfortable black couch stood on a square of granite tiles, and opposite it where a TV would normally go stood a massive bookshelf instead. But there were still signs here and there that Jesse was proud of his work, just not conceited. I noticed framed photographs of him with what I imagined were other cast members, some of which were covered in signatures, and he had a couple of posters from the show itself.

I tore myself away from the view and walked through the living room toward the bedroom, and along the way, I noticed a picture of a younger Jesse surrounded by a group of smiling people who all shared similar facial features. I paused to look at it and chuckled at what was obviously a family photo. Jesse clearly got his eyes from his mom, but he had his dad's hair.

"Almost ready over here!" Jesse called from the bedroom, and I made my way in to see what he had decided on for the night.

According to Jesse, the dress code for the evening was technically business casual, but the kind that didn't advertise that you were trying for business casual too hard. I hadn't been sure what he meant, so he had explained that it was like an unspoken middle ground between business casual and smart casual. That had only been more confusing, so we had just done a little shopping as soon as we arrived in L.A.

He was wearing dark blue pants with a striped red-and-white button-down and a bold maroon blazer, while my outfit was entirely black: black blazer, shirt, pants, and dress-casual shoes. Despite it all being black, Jesse had insisted that this particular outfit was made of matching blacks from a designer that would catch the eye but not too much, which I greatly appreciated.

However, the sight of Jesse in his clothes for the evening made me want to cancel on the party and spend an evening seeing how foggy I could make those windows all over the house. The look I gave Jesse when I appeared in the doorway said as much.

"I like this," I said, approaching him as he stood in front of a triple mirror and straightened his collar.

He smiled as I came up behind him to wrap my arms around him, and he leaned back on me when he felt my shaft growing between his tight cheeks.

"I cannot tell you how happy I was to find out that these sizes fit me again," he said, running his hand over the flat of his stomach. "Honestly, I just figured I was going to be stuck at that waist size forever now that I'm in my thirties."

"We've had a lot of time for cardio," I teased, squeezing his ass softly and making that smile of his take on a somewhat different undertone.

"I have you to thank for a lot of this, by the way," he said, looking at me in the mirror, and I chuckled.

"I wouldn't be doing jack if you didn't want it in the first place. Don't sell yourself short," I said. "But I think you always look good. And if you want proof of that, all you've gotta do is ask," I added, sliding my hands up and down his thighs and groping them shamelessly.

"God, you make it tempting to skip this thing," Jesse murmured as I kissed his neck and smelled fresh cologne on him, and he put his hand over mine, squeezing it.

"That would be a good way to start some drama," I said. "Interrupt your time away from all this to come to a party, only to rain check on it at the last minute."

Jesse snorted a laugh, and he turned to peck me on the cheek.

"That sounds too real," he teased. "I like how you think. How are you feeling about all this, by the way?"

Jesse had asked that question what felt like a hundred times, but I wasn't annoyed by it. I knew he just wanted to make sure I wasn't uncomfortable going far beyond what was being asked of me in my contract, but I knew we were way beyond that.

"You know, the more you ask, the more likely I am to just tell you I'm having second thoughts as we're walking through the doors," I said, and he laughed softly. "Honestly, the only thing I'd worry about is people giving us the side-eye for you being here with your bodyguard."

"Then maybe I don't have to introduce you as my bodyguard," he said after a moment's thought. "How about boyfriend?"

My heart skipped a beat, and a broad grin spread over my face as Jesse turned around to face me. I slipped my arms over his shoulders and loomed over him with a loving gaze, then kissed him softly on the lips.

"That sounds perfect," I said.

* * *

A COUPLE OF HOURS LATER, the limousine that Jesse's agent had insisted on us taking was dropping us off at a midsized manor that was designed to look like some kind of Mediterranean villa. I climbed out of the car first, then extended a hand to help Jesse out while looking at the mermaid fountain that stood in the middle of the brown cobblestone circular driveway.

This was the home of Anthony Bernard, someone who had at one point been something of a mentor-figure to Jesse and was nearing retirement age. To hear Jesse talk about him, he sounded like a legend in the soap opera world.

"Your friend is a man who knows what he likes, at least," I said, looking up at the palm trees wafting in the breeze and letting my gaze drift to the manor itself, where the lights and music from inside told us we had arrived at a perfect time.

"That he is," he said, straightening his blazer and waving to the driver. "Good to see Anthony hasn't changed much. Shall we?"

I expected to head inside, but instead, Jesse led me around toward the gate to what a normal house would call a backyard, but this manor held something altogether different. An ivy-covered wall blocked our view, and a doorman met us to check our invitations before opening the door with a smile and allowing us in.

Beyond was a garden party that had been arranged to look and feel like a villa's vineyard in the heart of Spain. The smell of chorizo in the air was unmistakable.

"Yes, he's serving tapas," Jesse said when he saw me take a deep breath with a warm smile. "And please, have everything you want to try. Don't let my eating regiment get in the way of your first time at an L.A. party. But I need to stay *far* away from the paella if I want to survive tonight," he said, laughing it off.

"If you're staying away from it, then your bodyguard isn't leaving you to pig out, either," I said with a gruff smile. "Nice try, but I'm not leaving you high and dry."

"You're not my bodyguard tonight, though; you're my boyfriend," he teased back with a defiant smirk.

"I could be both," I pointed out, crossing my arms and raising an eyebrow.

"Bodyfriend," Jesse said with a playful smile, seeing how the word combo sounded. "Sounds better than boyguard, so I'll take it."

We made our way toward an open-air courtyard where a trellis and wooden beams wrapped in vines provided the feeling of coverage in the space where most of the guests were mingling. There was a large pool further behind the manor where a number of people were swimming and chatting, but Jesse and I didn't have any interest in swimming unless we could play around with each other the way we always wanted to when we stripped down to nothing but our swim trunks.

I wasn't the type to keep up with celebrities, and most of the crowd here was probably involved with soap operas, but there were some faces it would be impossible not to recognize. They might have looked a little different than the faces I knew from their high-profile shows, thanks to the toned-down makeup, but they were people I had seen on TV, and it made the experience a little surreal if I was being honest.

What was more, most everyone we passed seemed to recognize Jesse, and they gave him passing smiles and waves as we walked. Some stopped him to give him a friendly hug and catch up for a few moments. These conversations almost always went exactly the same, which told me a good deal about how close these people actually were to Jesse:

"Oh, Jesse! So good to see you again. Glad you could make it! Where on earth have you been?"

"Just taking some personal time away from home," Jesse would say politely, "but I couldn't resist stopping by to catch up with Anthony."

"He's great, isn't he? By the way, are you slimming down for your next season? You look like you've been working out."

"A little, with my boyfriend Marshall's help," he would always say, diverting attention to me.

I would then exchange a brief handshake with another TV star and an even briefer greeting. The rich and famous weren't interested in me, and I knew that beforehand, so I wasn't jealous or offended in the slightest. In fact, I didn't half mind this. Jesse was getting recognition in all aspects of his life, and it made him feel good, nobody tried to bother me with small talk I couldn't possibly keep up with, and I got to enjoy the scenery while keeping an eye out so that I wasn't neglecting my job.

"Sorry we keep getting interrupted," Jesse said after another encounter, and we finally had a moment to slip over to the open bar. "I'm trying to find Anthony, but he can be elusive sometimes."

"I'm enjoying watching you soak up all the attention," I said sincerely. "Want a drink?"

"Oh, I do," he said with a longing gaze at the bar, where the bartender was smiling enticingly as she poured what looked like a Cosmo. "But I don't want to go crazy or anything. What's a low-calorie drink, anyway?"

"Gin and tonic is probably the 'best' as far as liquors go," I said, but Jesse was already grimacing.

"Not my favorite, but maybe they have flavored tonic water," he said.

"You could just get a drink you like and cut loose for the night," I suggested. "It *is* a party, after all."

"I know, but I want to try it," he said, approaching the bar. "They say try something you don't like once a year, right?"

"I'll try it if you do," I said, grinning at him. "I mean, I don't like the taste of pine-scented cleaner either, but good gin isn't bad."

"Deal," Jesse said, and I turned to the bartender.

"Couple of gin and Ts, with lemon tonic, if you have it."

A minute later, we clinked our glasses together and took swigs of the sour drink. Jesse's face contorted hilariously, and even I had to fight to keep from frowning and smacking my lips.

"Okay, not... as bad as I was expecting," Jesse started before laughing through the rest of the sentence.

"Pretty bad though," I said, nodding. "Want a different one?"

"No, we're committed now," Jesse insisted with a grin. "So help me god, I'm finishing this gin and tonic."

"Gin and mistake," I murmured before turning to the bartender. "This is a great drink, by the way, don't get us wrong."

"No offense taken. Can't stand the stuff either," the bartender admitted with a laugh before hurrying over to other guests.

"Jesse, there you are," came an older gentleman's voice from behind us.

We turned to see a well-dressed man in a blue-and-white tieless suit that showed a little more chest than it needed to, but the man wearing it carried himself with easygoing confidence. It was a similar vibe to Jesse's, I thought, but Jesse definitely wore it better.

"Anthony, look at you!" Jesse said, meeting his mentor's hug.

"Look who's talking," he said, looking Jesse up and down. "Look at you. Who says they can take the country out of the boy, eh?"

Jesse's cheeks burned at the compliment, and as I stood back with my arms crossed and my posture its usual stiff self, I couldn't help but smile. Jesse deserved this validation. He had come to Winchester for himself, not to impress his peers, but as far as I was concerned, this was icing on the cake for him.

If he was denying himself real cake, then I'd give him a double serving of the metaphorical type.

"Well, I've been taking some time to rein myself in," Jesse said, turning to me, "but a lot of that is thanks to my boyfriend, Marshall."

Anthony turned to me with a searching smile as he shook my hand, and he gave a charming nod that told me he liked what he saw.

"Ah," he said, "I was wondering where that spring in your step was coming from. A pleasure, Marshall."

"All mine," I said with a curt nod, and I followed the two of them as we sat down at a table by the wall to catch up.

Jesse and Anthony did most of the talking over the next twenty minutes or so, mostly about what I would expect—some ongoing work Anthony was up to, whether or not he would be retiring soon, a little gossip about their colleagues. I contributed here and there, but letting the two of them talk left me free to keep an eye on the party.

After some time had passed, the wine and liquor were starting to loosen up the partygoers, and the evening outside the little bubble we were in got gradually louder. More importantly, more people were showing up, and I didn't see as many security personnel moving around as I would have liked for a party of this size.

By the time Anthony was making his polite excuses to go see other party guests and we all began to stand up, I heard something peculiar. It was the shutter of a camera lens. I was sure I had heard it. But where had it come from? I scanned the crowds and saw nothing. Were my ears playing tricks on me? I didn't feel the slightest buzz from my drink.

"What's the matter?" Jesse asked after Anthony took his leave.

"We should probably go," I said, nodding to the door. "The party is starting to get a little wild. People might be migrating to the pool soon, and I don't know if I want to be swimming in champagne and spilled drinks."

"Good point," Jesse said, "I'll call the limo."

We made our way to the party's exit, and along the way, I quietly tipped off the doorman to give Anthony's security detail a heads-up that the party might have uninvited guests.

Spilling through the door to Jesse's apartment later that night had never felt better. We were already on each other's lips as we staggered inside and shut the door behind us, but we had started feeling each other up in the limo on the way over. I was surprised we had lasted as long as we did.

"Do you have any idea how good it feels to wade through a crowd knowing you have my back?" Jesse groaned in a break in the action as I worked his shirt buttons.

"As good as it felt to watch you get the appreciation you deserve," I said, throwing his shirt aside and pinning him to the door.

I lifted him by the ass and let him wrap his legs around my waist, then carried him to the couch as our shoes clattered to the ground one by one. His mouth was on my neck as I sat down with him, and our cocks were hard under the fabric of our pants.

"Now I'm going to show you everything I wanted to do at that villa," I growled into his ear as I felt a shiver run through his body.

JESSE

I HAD NEVER FELT THIS KIND OF EXHILARATION BEFORE. EVEN IF I HAD wanted to take the time to go through my old memories and remember some of the best things that had ever happened to me, the brightest and sweetest moments of my life thus far, none of them could possibly stand up to the feeling I got every time Marshall got close to me like this. It was a feeling of overwhelming joy and gratefulness that almost brought tears to my eyes.

I had never felt this way before. Not even when I first received the call informing me that I had won the coveted role of Adrian Bannister. Not even when I won a prestigious award in exchange for my portrayal of that character and was recognized on a near-global scale for my hard work and dedication. No award, no amount of money or fame or recognition could possibly compare to the simple joy of touching Marshall's glorious body.

I didn't want to waste a single second. I didn't want to close my eyes for even a moment in case I missed some subtle shift of his chest muscles or the flicker of adoring light shining in his eyes. My veins throbbed with adrenaline. My heart pounded like mad, like I was about to grab a parachute by the strings and free-fall out of a helicopter over a snow-covered mountain. And that was how it always felt: like I was on the brink of falling into some gorgeous abyss, twisted and glimmering with new dreams and new hopes for the future. That was what I saw when I looked up into Marshall's eyes as he hovered over me, touching and groping my body all over. I could never get enough. I knew without a shred of doubt that forever still wouldn't be a long enough time to discover all the things I could love and treasure about this amazing man. He inspired me in a way no script, scene, or swell of music ever could, and the most incredible part was that he didn't even have to try. Just by simply existing, by being himself, I was impressed beyond belief. He was a fascination to me, and being close with him felt like the most beautiful gift this world could ever offer me.

He had cradled me back onto the soft cushions of the living room sofa with such care that it almost stunned me into silence. I had taken my fair share of lovers to bed, but all of those experiences paled in comparison to the way it felt with him. Marshall was an angel on earth, something out of this world. I wondered if I would ever fully understand him. He revealed things about himself so very slowly, so cautiously, as though he was worried that he might slip up and show too much. Like he still had things to hide from me. As if I would not adore him just the same anyway. And I knew that, with every resounding thump-thump of my heart against his, it was true: no matter where he came from, no matter what he had done in the past, I would never get over him. I would never stop gazing at him with such potent desire and admiration. He was everything I'd never expected to find during my lifetime, especially not in a town like Winchester. Sometimes it blew my mind just thinking about how crazy the odds were stacked against us. How lucky was I to have returned to the sleepy, largely unknown town of Winchester in the first place? And then to actually follow through with my plan to take on a sabbatical for my own well-being? Something I had always scoffed at over the years, preferring to stick to a hard-and-fast schedule in the hopes of proving myself to my audience, to my costars and crew members that I was capital-S *Serious* about my work.

What were the odds that within the first twenty-four hours of arriving in this picturesque little corner of the world, I would cross paths with the man who would forever alter the course of my life and leave an indelible impression on my heart? How lucky could I have been to meet a man so opposite of me, and yet so uniquely, almost mystically compatible with my heart? There were moments when I looked at Marshall and I couldn't help but wonder, in the quiet depths of my soul: where did you come from? How did you find me when I didn't even know I needed you yet? And most importantly, how in the world can I find a way to keep you?

Because by now, I had no intention of giving him up. Not without a fight. I still had no idea how to do it, how to make this happen. But I knew I had to try. I knew I had to give breath to these hopes and dreams and try to help them take to the air. Maybe it would all come crashing down eventually. Maybe. But god, even if we crashed and burned in the long run, it would still be worth it. Without question. Without hesitation. I was his. And he was mine.

His lips crashed against mine, his tongue probing into my mouth as I moaned and arched my back, rolling my hips to meet his strokes. He was still fully clothed except for his shoes, but I was already shirt-less, feeling my nipples stiffen a little as the friction of his shirt fabric brushed against my bare chest. I felt him growl, low in his throat, as he dipped down to press passionate, bruising kisses along my sensitive collarbone. Every nip and graze of his teeth on my bare skin gave me goose bumps, the ticklish and delicious sensations flooding my body with exhilaration. Every minuscule movement, breath, or murmur from Marshall was enough to make me tremble with need. I had never longed for anything as badly as I craved his closeness. I needed it. My body was crying out for a release, for an outlet to express the buzzing feeling of intense fondness in my soul. I wanted him more than I had ever wanted anything before. We had done this so many times already and yet every time felt as thrilling and satisfying as the first.

"It was such a treat seeing you here in Los Angeles," I mumbled. "Watching you walk through a sea of famous people, totally oblivious."

"Hey now." He laughed gruffly, "I recognized some of them."

"I know, I know. I just meant that you were never intimidated. You're fearless, Marshall, and I admire that about you," I explained.

A smile played around his lips, never fully forming. But the softness in his gaze was more than enough to show me what he was really feeling. I was filled with pure awe and gratitude to be here with him right now.

"You know, there is truly nowhere else I would rather be right now than right here with you," I added quietly as he bent down to kiss my forehead. "Anywhere with you, really."

"I feel the same way. Los Angeles is not my kind of town, I have to admit. I was a little wary about coming here. This isn't my crowd. It isn't my comfort zone. It sure as hell ain't my climate," he joked gently. "But I can't help but feel like a piece of home has followed me and been beside me all this time: you."

I felt a momentary sting of happy tears burn in my eyes which I hastily blinked back. He was perfect. He knew just the right thing to say without overthinking it, without any guile whatsoever. Marshall didn't play mind games. He didn't toy with my heart and head the way some of my exes did. He was just who he was—straightforward, honest, real. All the time. It was so refreshing after years of dealing with uptight, flighty, two-faced people in Los Angeles. There was no pretending with Marshall. There was no smokescreen. He lived truthfully and inspired me to do the same.

And it was that thought which propelled me to do what I did next.

I reached up to cup his cheek in my hand, staring up lovingly into his dark eyes. He looked at me intently, like he knew I was about to say something important.

"Marshall, I don't know how I managed to find you. But damn, am I glad I did. Thank you," I said emphatically.

He looked ever so slightly confused, which only made him more adorable. "For what?" he inquired.

I smiled. "For being you. For being so real and genuine all the time. For going above and beyond to protect me. For coming to L.A. with me, even though it's not your scene at all," I said.

He raised an eyebrow and nuzzled the tip of his nose against mine.

"I'm doing my job, Jesse. I'm taking care of you. I wouldn't dream of making you go off on your own. It's not just that it's a job, though. It's...more than that," he murmured, almost more to himself than to me.

"What do you mean?" I asked softly. He looked into my eyes, thinking it over, measuring out his words.

Then he simply kissed me and said, "I like knowing you're safe. I like being the one to make sure of that. You have come to mean a lot to me, Jesse. You're important to me," he said gruffly.

I could tell this was a little difficult for him. He wasn't used to discussing such deep emotions with anyone, much less a fellow man. But it warmed my heart even more to see him opening up to me. Surely that meant I had to be doing something right. And if that were the case, I fully intended to keep doing exactly that.

"You're important to me, too," I replied in a low voice. "More than I can even explain."

"Sometimes words aren't quite enough," Marshall said sagely. "But actions... hopefully I can show you."

He leaned back on his knees and pulled off his suit jacket and shirt, tossing them over to the chair. I watched with rapt attention as he took off his pants. I held my breath when he bent over to pull off my pants and boxers. Then we were both naked and hard in the low light of the living room lamp. Marshall's massive cock throbbed and bounced as he moved closer to straddle me. He bent down to kiss me on the lips, then let his mouth trail down my cheek, my neck, my chest. His hands roved along my body as well, groping and feeling me up. I loved being manhandled by a big, powerful man like him. He was in full control of my body and what we did together. I'd always considered myself a fairly assertive, if not dominant, kind of man. But with Marshall everything was different. I trusted him implicitly. I knew he would never do anything to harm me. He knew what he wanted, but he also knew what I wanted, even without having to ask. When he slipped down between my thighs and began stroking my cock with one hand while he touched himself with the other, I nearly arched off the bed. I rolled my hips, meeting his every stroke. His palm was pleasantly, delightfully rough from years of working with his hands, and the friction of his hand against the velvety smooth skin of my shaft was unbelievable.

"Fuck, that feels so good," I whimpered breathlessly.

"I'm not done with you yet," he growled.

Once he had stroked me nearly to the edge, he bent to suck the head of my cock into his mouth. The sudden onslaught of slick warmth almost made me come, but Marshall was careful. He knew exactly what he was doing. He moved slowly up and down on my cock, applying just enough pressure to keep me hot and bothered without pushing me over the brink. I cried out and grasped at the sofa cushion, holding on for dear life. Marshall was determined to tease me out, pushing and pushing me closer, only to slow down and back away again. Soon, he used a squirt of lube to slick his fingertips, massaging the tight circle of muscle around my ass while he expertly sucked my cock. By the time he rolled a condom on over his throbbing shaft, I was damn near incoherent with desire. I bit my lip so hard I almost drew blood while he positioned the thick head of his cock at my opening and smoothly slid inside with one thrust. I cried out and grappled for purchase as he immediately began to pound my ass hard. I could tell he had been holding back for quite some time, too, and now there was little to stop him from giving me the ride of my life.

We rocked together fast and hard, the tip of his cock slamming deep inside me with every powerful thrust. He brushed against my sensitive prostate, making me tremble and groan with pleasure. But he wasn't finished with me yet.

He withdrew for just a moment, and I whimpered with disappointment. But then I looked up and saw the fire burning brightly in his dark eyes, and I knew I was in for a real treat.

"Turn around. On your stomach," he commanded roughly.

I did as I was told, flipping over and bracing myself on my knees. I felt and heard him give my bare ass a resounding smack, and I groaned, backing up against him. I glanced back over my shoulder to see him smirking devilishly, and then he pushed back inside of me—

hard. I yelped with deliciously mingled pain and pleasure, bouncing my ass against him while he slammed into my prostate again and again.

"You're incredible," he grunted. "Feels so fucking tight."

I was so wrapped up in waves of tingly pleasure I couldn't even form words. I just held on while the man of my dreams pummeled me from behind. I felt his hands grasp my hips, holding me in place while he fucked me faster and more erratically. He was starting to lose control, and so was I. Harder and harder, faster and faster he went until finally, in one massive moment of tension, we both seized up and came together. I felt his spunk thickly filling up the condom in my ass while I came all over the sofa cushion. That would be one hell of a stain to deal with, but at the moment I couldn't have cared less.

Marshall finally pulled out, and I turned over on my back. He collapsed beside me, the two of us barely able to fit together on the sofa. He pulled me into his arms, kissing me softly as we both basked in the afterglow. I never wanted this moment to end. Here, in his embrace, was the happiest place in the universe. That I knew for certain. After a while, we went to shower together before falling into bed. The final thought that crossed my mind before I drifted off to sleep was the surety that I was falling for Marshall.

* * *

THE NEXT DAY, we woke up and packed our belongings up in a rush, taking a taxi to LAX. After the wild night we'd had before, we were a little sluggish today and running slightly behind schedule for our flight. As usual, the airport was slam-packed with tourists and business people alike, all clamoring to queue up at the security check-ins and kiosks. Marshall and I were rushing through the gigantic airport, dragging our luggage along behind us. I had been late for flights before, but it never really got any less harrowing, no matter how many times I went through it. Luckily, though, I was with the most patient, even-keeled traveling companion imaginable. Even though I couldn't stop checking the clock and worrying that we would be too late and miss our flight altogether as we stood in the long check-in line, Marshall was calmer than Lake Wren. He exuded a sort of stoic peace about the whole thing. He knew there was no use in fretting over the minutes passing quickly by. There was not much we could do to avoid it.

"Shit. Why are people moving so slowly?" I whispered to him with annoyance.

He shrugged. "They're moving at a normal pace, Jesse. You're just stressed out."

I stared at him for a moment, stunned. "How on earth are you this calm right now? Are you not worried at all?" I asked.

He raised an eyebrow and put an arm around me warmly.

"Hey, we'll get there when we get there. Whether it's this flight or the next one. If it's the money you're worried about—" he began, but I cut him off.

"No, no. God, no. If we have to pay for a new flight, I'll do it. No problem. It's just... I hate the feeling of being rushed. It's that 'hurry-up and wait' thing that drives me up the wall," I hissed back. Marshall looked almost amused.

"Isn't that what your filming days are like, though? Shouldn't you be used to it?" he pointed out. I had to concede that he had a point there.

"Well, yeah," I confessed. "But it's different. I get paid for that."

Marshall laughed. "Fair enough. But seriously, don't sweat it. Airports are always hectic. Don't let it get to you," he advised wisely.

The rest of our time at the airport went slowly, but smoothly. I was eternally grateful to have Marshall beside me, as he moved like a gentle giant through the harried crowds. When we sat down at our gate just five minutes before boarding was supposed to begin, it hit me just how happy I felt. Despite the stress of being in LAX and everything that came along with it, I still felt amazing. I couldn't stop smiling. And I knew exactly why. Here, at the gate surrounded by crying children and grumpy travelers, was the most unromantic place in the world. And yet, my heart still swelled with warmth. I couldn't stop looking up at the gorgeous, stoic man beside me and thinking just how lucky I was to be here—to be anywhere—with him. He made me feel grounded and floating at the same time. He gave me strength, but he also made me vulnerable. He reined me in but built me up, too.

I realized, as we stepped into line to board our flight, that maybe I had been a little misguided when I picked Winchester to go on sabbatical. Maybe my reasoning was off. I wasn't in search of my roots. I was looking for a loving and honest man to go through life with.

And maybe, just maybe, if I got lucky... I could say that I'd found him.

MARSHALL

AFTER A TRIP TO L.A. AND BACK ON SUCH SHORT NOTICE, FIGHTING through a few of the airports in the world at peak vacation season, and staggering back to Winchester after it was all said and done...a few days of relaxation were more than welcome. A few days after our flight brought us back to Charleston and we drove back to Winchester, we were enjoying one of those "recovery days" with a cozy dinner in together. At around eight, we were sitting on the couch in the living room, leaning against each other as the night wound down.

Two empty plates sat on the coffee table before us, bearing the remains of what had been tofu tacos a few moments ago. They were a very simple recipe that Carter had sent me after the barbecue—one of about a dozen recipes, in fact. I had no idea how the guy found time to cook like that on top of his job, but damn, the man knew his way around a kitchen.

I wasn't about to pretend that I could cook better than Jesse, who at least knew the basics of what healthy cooking involved. But I wanted to try my hand in the kitchen, and Jesse had been more than happy to indulge that urge.

Tofu tacos hadn't exactly inspired me with hope when I heard the name, but Carter's guide to making tofu work gave us results that were good enough that we were both too full for seconds. Carter had specified that I needed extra firm tofu, first of all. That kind apparently worked well for recipes where tofu was being used as a meat substitute because it could be worked into a similar texture and flavor as chicken. I then had to press the tofu and dry it with a little salt, then marinate that in a concoction of a hell of a lot of spices and some olive oil for most of the day. Learning that made tofu make a little more sense to me: it was a blank slate I could put just about any flavor into with enough time. Between the tofu and the basic pico recipe he included, we had a surprisingly satisfying and very spicy trio of corn tortilla tacos each.

Jesse was reading while the stereo was playing relaxing music for the evening, and in the meantime, I was on my laptop, scrolling through a few sports websites to look into a new set of paddles for the canoe. My old ones were fine, but they were starting to show their age.

"Oh my god," Jesse murmured, distracting me.

I looked over to see that he was glancing down at his phone with an apprehensive look on his face, and his eyes flitted up to mine and quirked an eyebrow.

"Looks like we dodged that party at Anthony's at the right time," he said, handing his phone to me, which had an article pulled up on it from a tabloid-adjacent site.

The headline showed pictures that were definitely from the house party we had been to, but it looked like it was much later in the night than we had stayed around for. There were a lot of familiar faces together, most of them in rosy-cheeked states of drunk. The article itself was a mildly embarrassing piece that boiled down to a "gotcha" moment of all those celebrities just behaving like people did at parties. It even listed a few names, but Jesse's was not among them, thankfully. I fought a smile off my face as I scrolled through the pictures.

"Damn, that's a shame," I said, handing him back the phone. "I'd say 'at least they had a good time', but I think I prefer how we spent the rest of the night."

"I'd say so, yeah," Jesse teased, squirming closer to me as I went back to scrolling through some shopping.

But while I was scrolling, another icon on my screen blinked at me.

"The fuck?" I murmured quietly, furrowing my brow and pulling it up.

"What's up?" Jesse asked, lowering his e-reader and peering over at me.

"One of the cameras outside picked up on something big," I said, standing up and shoving my phone into my pocket. "Big enough to trip the sensor, but whatever it is only got a blurry half shot caught on camera. I'm going out to see what it is."

"Are you sure?" he asked, sitting up on the couch and looking worried. "I don't want you to get hurt out there."

"I'm still your bodyguard, remember?" I said, leaning down to peck him on the cheek, which earned me a smile.

"Just be careful!" he called after me as I slipped into a pair of moccasin-slippers and a flashlight, then headed outside.

The warm, humid night air hugged my body closely as I hurried out across the grass in the direction of the camera that had picked up on the motion. We hadn't had anyone try to actually intrude on the property yet, so something about the audacity of trying it after all this time got under my skin—especially on a night where I was enjoying an otherwise nice time not worrying about anything else in the world. With that in mind, I had a little more energy than usual carrying me out to the tree line. Protecting Jesse felt good, plain and simple.

Besides, after doing this job for almost a full month and not having to help Bill out of The Chisel for so long, I was missing the feeling of escorting someone off the premises. I wasn't too picky about which premises.

The beam of light from my flashlight roved over the tree line as I approached, and I heard rustling, but the light didn't pick up on anything. I moved it around in a broader circle, even checking some of the yard—there was a chance an intruder had slipped past me and kept low in the darkness. There was a lot of cloud coverage tonight, so the shadowy darkness was working against me. But a fully-grown man ought to have still been fairly easy to spot if he was careless enough to get caught by my cameras.

I stopped moving so I could listen, and finally, the rustling of leaves drew my attention not to eye level, as I was expecting, but upward. I shone my flashlight into a tree, and my eyes widened at the sight of...the biggest, fattest raccoon I had ever seen in my life.

We stared at each other for a few seconds to the sound of crickets in the background. I turned the light away from its face, and as its luminous, reflective eyes dimmed, I watched it hunker down and try to make itself more hidden among the branches. My phone was connected to the notification system on my laptop, so I pulled up the picture that the motion detection had caught and compared the blurry half blob to the raccoon in front of me.

"Perfect match," I murmured with a smile up at the critter. "You need a cab? Think you've had a few too many."

The raccoon didn't reply, but I got the vibe that it was vaguely indignant, probably.

"All right, you're off the hook, but I've got my eye on you," I warned it jokingly, then turned and walked back to the house.

I swiped the notification off my screen and smiled at my overprotectiveness. I'd all but raised the alarm over a raccoon. I couldn't help but feel overprotective of Jesse, though. The guy liked seeing himself as a down-to-earth person so much that I thought he sometimes walked into danger too often. And a brave raccoon could be more of a threat than some people realized, after all—if we'd had a bag of marshmallows anywhere in the house, it would have been toast, I thought with a soft laugh.

I turned off my phone screen, but then it lit up again with an incoming call. My brow furrowed. Who the hell had reason to call me at this hour? My first thought was that something had happened at The Chisel that they needed emergency help for, but I didn't recognize the number on the screen.

"Hello?" I grunted in answer.

"Sounds like you haven't changed a bit," said my uncle's voice.

I stopped dead in my tracks, feeling my body tense. I hadn't heard from my uncle since I packed my bags in Atlanta and rode off in my truck. And in all honesty, I didn't think I would have minded not hearing from him for a good, long time after that.

"Warren," I said, not hiding the gruffness in my voice as I heard the sound of a cigarette getting sucked on over the receiver. "Long time."

"That's one way of putting it, sure," he said. "How the hell have you been, Marshall?"

He was acting friendly, which told me he probably wanted something. I had grown up hearing him call my mom—his sister—and have long conversations over the phone that usually had her expression turning sour, but just when Mom was ready to start giving him the cold shoulder, he'd warm up enough to remind us that he was family, and that was that. He had always been a complicated character before I went to work with him, and what I'd figured out about him in Atlanta told me plenty about who he really was.

"Been all right," I said, pacing toward the lake slowly. "Living life slow and steady. Took Mom out for her birthday."

"Oh, damn, that was last week, wasn't it?" he said in a tone that didn't sound especially concerned about having forgotten his sister's birthday. "I'll have to send her a late card."

"Week before last," I corrected him. "How've you been? Where are you at, these days?"

I tended to let my dialect get heavier when I was talking to people I had known for as long as my uncle.

"Still down here in Hotlanta," he said cheerfully. "Takes more than one business going under to get me down. You oughta know that."

"Oh yeah?" I asked, trying not to let the concern in my voice show. "Whatever happened with the nightclub? I got a little caught up in moving and the new job."

"That old place? Shit, I half forgot about it," he said, laughing it off. "Just didn't take off. Looked like it wasn't going to hold out for another year, so I sold it off and pocketed a modest profit. Nothing special. Been working my way through the city on a few new projects I'm working on."

That was a flat-out lie, and I knew it. But I wasn't about to call him out on it, because the way he worded that answer told me he may or may not have known about the last few things I'd done before leaving Atlanta in such a hurry. The fact that he hadn't seemed to mind me not giving my two weeks made me uneasy, too. And I was pretty sure he knew that, which annoyed me even more.

"Good to hear you're doing well for yourself, then," I said vaguely, trying to steer this into a routine family call I could keep brief. "What's up?"

"Well now, no need to rush. It's been a while since we've talked," he said. "Actually, I was wondering how you've been doing for yourself since you decided the nightclub life wasn't working out for you."

There it was. Warren had a way of hedging his words, both compliments and insults. And he was always leading you somewhere with anything he was saying. But two years was a long time, and I told myself privately to give him the benefit of the doubt. That was what Mom always did. I decided to ignore the guarded question about why I had left and focus on the rest.

"No complaints," I said honestly, glancing back at the house where I figured Jesse was probably wondering about me. "I'm running personal security for a big name who's laying low for a while. Can't talk about the job too much, but I'm enjoying it."

Warren gave a low whistle over the phone.

"Sounds like you're babysitting a big shot, huh?" he said. "Bet they pay you well to keep you happy. You don't have to tell me what all that entails. I know you've got a handle on it. You were the best head of security I could have hired. Really wish I could have kept you in Atlanta for a little while longer. I could have hooked you up with some good connections here after the nightclub went under."

"It's not bad at all," I replied. "The guy's pretty great, I've gotta say. I came in expecting him to be a pain in the ass, but half the time, I forget I'm even on the job."

I still did my job, of course. It just felt like doing it for someone I cared for rather than someone I was being paid to help.

"Oh, don't let 'em fool you with the chummy act," he said in a dismissive tone. "They're all like that, those types who need body-guards. They know that good security is harder to replace than, say, serving staff, so they treat them nice and get better service out of them for less money. He's just a sweet-talker. Probably a politician or a musician or something, right? Someone with a lot of natural charisma?"

I didn't reply at first, because what Warren was saying had taken me off guard.

"Thought so," he followed up quickly. "Yeah, listen, do yourself a favor and don't get too attached. Types like that don't give a shit about whatever big lug they have watching their asses. They just want to get smashed on martinis in peace."

"I'll have to take your word for that," I said noncommittally, frowning.

"Do. It'll save you some headaches when your contract runs out, and he starts *'promising'* to renew it," he said, putting emphasis on the word to suggest that it wouldn't happen. "Funny you should bring all this up, actually. I wanted to call and see what you had on your plate right now because I've got a new business in Atlanta that's gonna need some security, and I need someone I *know* will do a solid job. When does this contract with Mr. Fancy-Pants end?"

I was so taken aback by what Warren sounded like he was saying that I couldn't think of a lie fast enough.

"Uh... not much longer now. Technically about a week," I said.

As I said it, I couldn't ignore the fact that my heart had sunk a bit at that thought. Time had flown by so fast that I'd barely registered that the steady march of time was bringing my contract to an end. The contract had come with a signing bonus that would let me take some time off to job hunt in case I didn't feel like going back to The Chisel immediately, but Jesse and I really hadn't taken much time to talk about how our relationship would affect that. Sure, the way we were talking, I thought it might be safe to assume we were staying together afterward, but I didn't have any guarantees of that. I couldn't have let myself get so caught up in the rush of our romance that I'd fooled myself, could I?

"Well, if that ain't serendipity, I don't know what is," he said brightly. "Here's the deal. I've bought a warehouse after cutting a great deal with a friend of mine who runs a shipping company. It's some kind of valuable tech hardware, so I'll need tight security to keep an eye on it. This kind of thing is like a magnet for thieves, but it's a hell of a lot easier to keep under control than a nightclub. And leagues better than anything you'll get to do in Winchester," he added.

"I don't remember saying I was still in Winchester," I said mildly.

"Nah, but you're a predictable guy, Marshall," Warren said matter-of-factly. "Ain't nothing wrong with that. Besides, if you hadn't headed back there, your mom would have started calling me and asking about you. I know it can't be all sunshine and roses up there. I remember what that town is like. All that fake Southern charm—they probably look at you like the traitor who went off to the big city like it was some den of vice, right?"

"It's not that bad," I said, and that was true enough, but I couldn't help but think back to the way some of the patrons at The Chisel regarded me at arm's length.

There was a pause on the line.

"I hear you," my uncle said at last. "Anyway, if you change your mind, the offer and the fifty grand starting salary it comes with is on the table. Just give me a call on this phone."

My jaw dropped. Fifty grand was a hell of a lot for security personnel, unheard of even. That was far more than I'd be able to land after this job with Jesse ended, assuming I didn't keep working for him professionally. Unless I got another personal security gig with a high-profile celebrity like him, I wasn't going to see that kind of money or stability anytime soon.

"Hold on. *Starting?*" I asked. "Where the hell is that kind of money coming from?"

"I told you, I cut a good deal," he said, laughing. "Told you a dozen times when you lived here, nobody bounces back like me, kid. But hey, don't get me wrong. Milk this security thing as much as you can. Just don't fool yourself into thinking it's more than a flash in the pan, seriously. Bodyguard work ain't stable like this would be. I know you're probably not gonna take my word for that since you're still young, but I'll be reviewing applicants for another couple weeks at least, so just mull it over, yeah?"

"Yeah," I said after a pause. "Sure, Warren."

"That's the Marshall I know," he said, and I could hear his grin through his voice. "Tell your mom I said hi."

He ended the call, and I stared down at the phone in my hand for a few moments in disbelief. To say I had mixed feelings about my uncle would have been an understatement. Our history together was long, but no matter what, he seemed to be able to pop in and out of my life at the drop of a hat as if we were the oldest and best of friends. If there was one thing I could say about him, it was that he had always been there for me...when it served his interests, but that was more than I could say about anyone else I'd met while working for him.

I wasn't about to take him at face value when he said all that about Jesse's kind of people. That attitude might have been true of some of the folks we met at the party, but not my Jesse. Right? I shrugged the thought off and walked back toward the house.

But even as I stepped through the kitchen door, something told me those thoughts were going to make it hard to sleep tonight—especially considering the uncertainty approaching on the horizon.

"Hey," Jesse said as soon as I was back. "Everything okay? You were gone for a while. Oh my god, was it that same photographer again?"

"No," I said in the straightforward tone I had used so much at The Chisel. "Just a raccoon. Got a call from an old friend who wanted to say hello," I lied, not wanting to worry Jesse.

He didn't need all my dirty laundry from Atlanta. He had enough to worry about on his own.

I was surprised to see him with the TV on, and even more surprised to see an episode of *Bannister Heights* playing. I walked up behind the couch and leaned on the back, smiling at the sight of Jesse on screen.

"I know, I know, it looks vain," he said, tilting his head back to look up at me. "But it's an episode from the latest season we filmed, and one of the actresses texted me insisting I needed to watch. We got some fabulous acting from some of the newer cast members, so I'm not watching for me, promise," he said. "Besides, we start filming the next season week after next, so I need to get back into the headspace of my character."

"Uh-huh," I said absently, watching the screen and trying not to think too hard about the prospect of Jesse going back to filming.

Jesse's character Adrian Bannister was holding a woman in his arms on the roof of a penthouse with a gorgeous view of a mountain range in the distance—or a very convincing fake set—and speaking to her in a passionate, hungry tone that I was surprised made it on screen. I had to admit, hearing Jesse's voice like that made my cock twitch. I couldn't hold back a smile when I noticed Jesse start to speak along with himself on screen, reciting his lines.

"I can't stand another night apart," he said, giving his character a playful smirk before looking up to me with lidded eyes, speaking the lines to me instead. "You light my skin on fire and keep me up thinking about you. That night after the ball, I should have stolen you away to England or France and gotten a summer home, just the two of us—and everything we've always wanted to say to each other," he added in a husky, suggestive tone.

Adrian the character finished his monologue by kissing his lover passionately, but Jesse the man waggled his eyebrows, even though he was only half joking. He reached up for me, and I bent down smiling to kiss him on the cheek, but I drew back before he could try to coax me onto the couch with a kiss on my neck.

He looked a little confused that I had drawn back, so I let my smile turn softer.

"Been a long day," I said. "Think I'd rather get an early night in and hit the sack to get an early start tomorrow."

"Oh, that sounds good too!" Jesse said cheerfully after a brief look of worry crossed his features.

It wasn't like me to steer away from sex, but everything Warren had told me had taken me far out of the mood. I wasn't sure what to think, except that my emotions had been pulled out like taffy, and the last thing I wanted to do right then was try to clear my head enough for sex.

Clearing my head at all was going to be a challenge, and for once, it wasn't one I was looking forward to.

JESSE

I WAS PACING BACK AND FORTH ON THE BACK DECK OF THE LAKE HOUSE, my phone wedged between my shoulder and my ear as I watered the plants with a vintage metal watering can kept in the shed at the back left corner of the property. With a stay as long as the one I was taking, the rental instructions had encouraged me to care for the potted plants from time to time. And because my agent was nothing if not ill-timed, he had managed to call me right in the middle of this little chore. But I was okay with it—I had been meaning to talk to him for a few days and discuss what the plan was going to be moving forward. It was a lovely day, cloudy but relatively warm. Lake Wren was smooth and glassy on the surface, reflecting the pale silvery clouds moving slowly overhead. The trees swayed in the breeze, and birds tweeted cheerily as they flitted from one branch to the next. It was another day in my private, quiet little corner of small-town paradise, and I had to admit it was a bit of a culture clash, looking out over the gorgeous rural landscape while fielding a phone call from my very citified, type-A agent. He had a sort of frenetic energy about him, like many other people who lived in Los Angeles. It was kind of funny, actually—people tended to think of California as the land of chilled-out surfers and sun-worshippers without a care in the world. And maybe there were parts of the state where you could, indeed, find that kind of California resident in droves.

But L.A. was not that kind of town. Everybody I knew back home ranged from slightly high-strung to full-on neurotic in varying degrees. My agent, Robert "Bobby" Wright, was one of the latter types. Granted, it wasn't entirely his fault. The life of a Hollywood agent was generally packed with lots of high-stress meetings to take, difficult deals to negotiate, and more often than not, flighty and demanding clients to appease. Everything in show biz was a negotiation, which was the main reason I kept Bobby employed on retainer. I loved the fast-paced atmosphere of being on set. Hell, I even thrived on the excitement and nervousness of attending casting calls and trying to impress the board. But the part I despised more than anything else, more than the long hours and high level of public scrutiny, was the business side of things. I hated having to advocate for higher pay. I detested the feeling of walking into a board room to lay down the law and break someone else down in the process when my agent needed me—and I wouldn't dream of leaving him high and dry with that job. That part always felt a little dirty to me, even though I knew full well it was just part of the Hollywood machine.

Still, I was lucky to have discovered Bobby. He was pretty well known and respected in the soap opera community, as he had worked with over two hundred actors and actresses in the field since he first got started in the early '80s. In fact, it was Anthony who had first introduced me to Bobby, as the agent had been working for my mentor at the time. In my opinion, you couldn't find higher praise than working for Anthony. His career was legendary, his filmography vast and impressive. So Bobby came to me highly recommended, although I had to admit that after weeks of living a calmer pace of lifestyle here in Winchester, it was startling to have to readjust to Bobby's quick-talking style of conversation.

I needed to talk to him, though. It was important. I had something pressing on my mind.

"Bobby, slow down. You don't have to give me the complete play-by-play," I said, pinching the bridge of my nose with frustration.

"But don't you want to know how the meeting went with the board? I put together one hell of a portfolio on your behalf and let me tell you, those guys ate it all up," he was rambling along at top speed.

I could hardly even keep track of what meeting he was talking about. In our world, there was always another meeting to attend, another contract to negotiate. I assumed it had something to do with my recurring role on Bannister Heights, which was of course my front-and-center role at the moment. But I had shot some small-time commercials and ads over the years, too. I tended to kind of forget about them the moment I walked off the set, as they took up so little of my time and effort. That was where Bobby came in, to keep it all organized and flowing together well.

"Well, thank you for that. I'm sure you did an amazing job," I said quickly.

"Thanks, man. Good to be appreciated," Bobby remarked. "Hey, how's the weather there? Not balmy and warm, I imagine."

"It's cloudy," I answered, and before I could say anything else, he kept going.

"Cloudy? Pfft. See, I don't get why you didn't jet off to Hawaii or something instead. Why South Carolina? No beaches, no babes in bikinis. I don't get it, man," he mused aloud.

"Well, first of all, I'm not at all interested in bikini babes," I pointed out.

"Yeah, yeah. Fair point. You're gay. But you can still appreciate the female form, eh? I mean, how can you not?" he went on, guffawing to himself.

I rolled my eyes. "I get enough of pretty, scantily clad people— male and female alike—back in Los Angeles. We already live at the beach, Bobby. I wanted something different," I said.

"Sure, all right. I get you," he said, definitely not getting me at all. "Anyway, how's it working out over there? You feeling refreshed and ready to come back to L.A. yet? Hollywood misses you. Everybody on the *Heights* team has been emailing me constantly, asking when you'll be back in town."

"I will be back soon enough. Before you know it. For now, I'm just trying to make the most of the time I've got left here," I explained. "But Bobby, there's something I wanted to discuss with you. It's important."

"Oh, really? Should I be worried?" he asked.

I couldn't help but smile. So typical.

"No, no. It's nothing bad," I assured him hastily. "I just… you know how I hired that guy to be my security detail while I'm here in Winchester?"

"Uh-huh. I still don't know why you wouldn't let me just fly out somebody here. God knows Los Angeles has more bodyguards looking for work than we know what to do with," he sighed with exasperation.

"I already explained I wanted to hire locally because—oh, it doesn't matter. Anyway, I really like this guy, okay? He's an amazing boy—bodyguard. He's gone above and beyond to keep me safe and defend my privacy while I'm on break," I explained to him, trying not to let my emotions slip through.

"All right. Good to know. You want me to work out a bonus for the guy for when you let him go and come back to L.A.?" Bobby assumed.

"No. Well, yes. He deserves a bonus, for sure. But that's not what I'm talking about right now," I said. I paused to take a breath, then went on. "I want to hire him again."

"Okay...so you're planning on going back to Winchester again?" he asked, sounding a little confused as to why I would ever want to come back here to South Carolina.

"Maybe. But I was thinking it might be a good idea to find a way to… to hire him back at home, too," I finally broached the subject.

There was a pause.

"Sorry, what?" Bobby asked.

"You heard me. This guy is phenomenal, Bobby. He's exceptional at his job. I've never felt safer and more secure than I do with him," I gushed.

"Huh. You sure it's his security skills that have you all worked up or is it something else?" my agent pointed out emphatically.

I winced, realizing that I had accidentally let some of my true feelings shine through. I needed to walk it back and make my pitch sound more practical.

"It's just a practicality thing, you know? I know you can appreciate a guy who does his work at a high level of excellence, being one such guy yourself," I said, laying it on thick.

I could almost hear him puffing out his chest with pride through the phone long-distance. Luckily, Bobby had a weakness. Flattery could get you pretty much anywhere with him. Hell, that was how I'd convinced him not to have a massive breakdown about my taking some time off out of state in the first place.

"But you don't need a bodyguard here in L.A., do you?" Bobby brought up.

"Well, no. Not me. But surely there are other people in Hollywood who could use an exceptionally talented and dedicated security guy, right? Somebody will want to hire him there. You've got every important celebrity's contact information. I know you do," I said.

"Yeah, that's my job, Jesse. Where are you going with this?" he asked with a sigh.

"What I'm asking is for you to find someone. Anyone. Somebody who needs a security guy, someone to hire him in Los Angeles. I just think he could really make a good living for himself out there, and I want to help him move forward in his career, you know?" I explained.

"You sound awfully invested in some rando bodyguard's future," Bobby said suspiciously. "Why the sudden interest in helping this guy? Are you really that bored over there in South Carolina? Or is there something else going on you're not telling me about?"

Damn, he was quick on the uptake.

"No, no. It's nothing weird. I just think he deserves more than what he's currently getting, okay? He's a good man. A good, solid worker. You would like him, Bobby. You really would," I said, totally sure of that fact.

"Maybe so, but that doesn't mean he should uproot his whole life and fly out to Los Angeles to work as a security guy," he pointed out. "Have you even asked him if he wants to do something like that? He's a local guy there, yeah?"

"Mhm. Born and raised," I said softly.

"All right, then. He's got roots there. Family. Friends. He probably has no interest in moving to L.A., Jesse. Besides, if you like him so much, why wouldn't you just try and keep him on for your own use?" he asked.

"Because," I groaned, "I don't want to be his boss anymore."

"Why not? I thought you said he was a great worker. What's the issue?"

I sighed, shaking my head. I didn't want to have to get into the nitty-gritty detail about why I wanted someone else to hire Marshall. I didn't want to explain that I desired a change in our dynamic. Being his boss seemed wrong to me at this point. We had moved far beyond the usual boundaries of employer and employee. Even beyond friendship. What was blossoming between Marshall and me was something genuine and authentic. Something monumental. I could no longer ignore it or push it aside. I could no longer just pretend that my feelings for him would somehow disappear once I left Winchester and returned home to Los Angeles. I couldn't lie to myself about the powerful feelings of intimacy and desire I felt for him. I didn't want to be his boss anymore.

I wanted to be his boyfriend. Officially. With no strings attached. With no quickly approaching date of separation and the awkwardness of his being on the payroll hovering over us like dead weight. I wanted to be free to touch him and adore him the way my heart felt the need to do. I wanted to love him, openly and without worry that someone might call it impropriety or an abuse of my position of power. Though that last concern was almost laughable to me considering how, even though I was the one employing Marshall, he was most definitely, without a doubt, the one calling the shots in our dynamic. Still, I knew that on paper, it wouldn't look good for me to be dating a guy who was here originally for just a paycheck. It had snowballed into something so much more, and I felt strongly that this burgeoning relationship, whatever it was, deserved better than our current arrangement.

But right now I had no good way to explain any of this to Bobby.

Not without revealing my deepest feelings about Marshall. And although I had known Bobby for years and shared a lot of secrets with him during that time, I still didn't want to discuss something so precious as this with him without first broaching the subject with Marshall himself.

"I mean, you said it yourself. I don't need a bodyguard in L.A., but someone else will. Listen, Bobby, it's important to me. Just promise you'll put out some feelers and see if you can find anyone else to take him on," I urged him.

Bobby groaned, and I could picture him rolling his eyes. "I'll keep my eyes open for an opportunity if one presents itself, but I think the more important thing is that you focus on preparing to come back here and get back into the swing of things, man. I know you're having a good time out there, although I can't figure out how, but your life is here. In Los Angeles. And it's time for you to take it back," he insisted.

"All right, all right. I got it," I said. "I will, but only if you say you'll do your best to find someone else to hire Marshall Hawkins. I don't want to be his boss anymore."

"Sure thing, Jesse. I'll try my best," Bobby relented, just as I heard the telltale scrape of the sliding glass door moving behind me.

Bobby hung up, and I swiveled around to see that Marshall was standing behind me on the deck, the door having just been slid shut. I gave him a broad smile, pleased as usual to see him, but he only gave me a cursory, cold glance. My heart sank as it dawned on me that he must have overheard something about my wanting to no longer be his boss.

What if he had taken it the wrong way?

"What was all that about?" Marshall asked gruffly.

"Oh, my agent called to chat," I said.

"Uh-huh," he said, still staring down at the wooden deck.

Still, I could tell he was expecting for me to explain in more detail. But I couldn't do it. I clammed up. I didn't want to mention the idea of someone hiring him on in Los Angeles unless I could present him with something tangible. I didn't want to lead him on a wild goose chase. But evidently, my answer wasn't enough for him. He shrugged and walked off without saying another word, leaving me to stand on the deck feeling totally confused. I didn't understand why he was suddenly acting *this* cold and detached. And when I really thought about it, I realized this wasn't an entirely new development. Marshall had been distant the past few days. We hadn't had sex, and he had been short and curt with me in conversation. He was acting more and more like the way he was when we first met weeks ago, and I didn't get why.

That night, as we sat at the table across from one another, eating dinner, he asked a question that totally threw me for a loop.

"Have you made arrangements for leaving yet?" he asked tersely, not even looking up from his plate.

I stared at him for a moment. "Oh. Uh, not really. I haven't even thought about it, to be perfectly honest," I said.

He nodded slowly. "Well, then, you might want to get on that," he replied.

Suddenly, my appetite had disappeared entirely. I set down my fork and just looked at him, wishing he would meet my gaze for even a second. I couldn't understand why he wanted to get rid of me so badly. I had expected that he would be trying anything and everything to prolong my time here so we could stay together longer, but that didn't seem to be the case. I couldn't help but feel a little hurt and confused. Had I done something wrong? Why did he suddenly want me out? As I excused myself from dinner to head upstairs and shower off before bed, I wracked my brain for a reason. Maybe he simply wasn't ready to leave Winchester yet, and he was trying to make a clean break. But then... something about that seemed wrong. There was something else going on here, even if I couldn't put my finger on it just yet.

MARSHALL

TODAY DIDN'T FEEL RIGHT, BUT IF THERE WAS ONE THING LIFE HAD taught me over the years, it was that those transitory moments in life never felt the way you wanted them to. And at almost one month on the dot since I had started working for Jesse, time was up, and I had been feeling like shit since I woke up this morning.

Jesse had gotten notice that he needed to head back to L.A. sooner than he had expected, and that day was today. Seeing the lake house in this state was the worst of all. From the time we got up to now, most of the day had been spent packing up Jesse's things and getting it all ready to roll.

He wasn't the only one packing up, either. Jesse's time renting the lake house was over, but even though he had a few more weeks left that he had paid for and invited me to make use of, I wanted to go ahead and get my stuff out of here. It wouldn't be the same without Jesse around.

I had never bothered moving my stuff out of the guest room and into Jesse's master bedroom, even though I'd spent every night with him, but it had only taken me a few minutes to pack up my clothes into the same bags I'd first brought over. I carefully folded the outfit Jesse bought me for the party, stifling the emotions that the look of them stirred up. I didn't expect to be shopping anywhere fancy anytime soon, so I wanted to save it, sentimental value aside.

I started to head down the stairs, but as soon as I took the first step, I saw Jesse appear at the bottom of them, about to come back up to his bedroom to keep packing. We both started to move out of the way, but Jesse nodded to me to walk down first.

"Moving days always sneak up on me, even when they aren't on short notice," Jesse said with a soft laugh, and I murmured an acknowledgment in return.

Jesse and I had been more distant over the past few days than we had been before. Ever since that phone conversation with my uncle, a whole slew of reality checks had come in to rain on the parade of what the past few weeks had been. Even though I wasn't about to buy into every word the man had said... they had given me pause, and Jesse's exit plans were only making me more uneasy. I didn't like what I overheard him say on the phone the other day, and even though I had been telling myself I had probably just heard something come out the wrong way...it was hard to buy that, in the big picture.

"So, are you sure you don't want to stay here a while?" he asked. "Still plenty of time. You might enjoy a few days to yourself for a change."

"Yeah," I grunted. "I'll take a few days to move the workout equipment back home, but I should get back. Need to get all the security equipment down too. I'm sure the owner of this place would appreciate me leaving it, but it's good equipment. I'll send it up to your place in case you want to use it again."

"Oh! Thanks, I hadn't even thought about that," Jesse said. "Yeah, but they might not enjoy accidentally setting off a tripwire outside," he added jokingly.

Jesse hung back at the bottom of the stairs as I walked past him, and I felt his eyes on my back as I headed out the door, carrying my stuff to my truck. I didn't like feeling like a problem, and Jesse's obvious awareness of the tension in the air sure as hell didn't help shake that feeling. He knew I suspected something was up, but he didn't want to say anything. All that just made it even more convincing that he was probably just quietly getting ready to forget about me as soon as he landed in L.A. I didn't want to let my imagination take me anywhere too melodramatic, but I had to face the real possibility that this was just a summer fling for Jesse.

There was just enough evidence to put me on the fence about it, and I hated being on the fence. He seemed to like me, and I didn't think any of our time spent in bed together was meaningless. People had short relationships like that all the time, right? But on the phone with his agent, he had sounded like he didn't want me working for him, and if that were the case, I couldn't imagine him giving me the highest praise to anyone else.

No, what I imagined might happen is that he'd give me a bunch of empty promises, head back to his home, and I'd suddenly slip his mind a few weeks later. That was probably the worst-case scenario, I told myself. Jesse was still a good guy. I wouldn't let myself think ill of him just because he was leaving. Best-case scenario, he was being honest about it all, but that didn't change the fact that he was about to start filming again, and it would probably be naïve of me to think that wouldn't distract him in a big way. I could see a middle ground working out—maybe he really would pass my name along to some security company, and I'd end up bouncing around L.A. for a while doing all kinds of security jobs. That didn't sound too bad.

But it was all still hypothetical, and I didn't want to ask Jesse about it *now* of all times, when it would make me look like the one who was just using him for a job opportunity. And on the flip side... my uncle's job offer in Atlanta was looking like a very solid alternative. He had his demons, sure, but it was nothing I couldn't handle long enough to save up some money and find better work in the area.

I had the foreshadow of a headache by the time I reached the truck and tossed my stuff in the back. I didn't like having to think about this kind of thing. I was a person who acted, not a person who got wrapped up in his own head. Funny that Jesse was the professional actor between us.

It was only another hour of packing and checking around the place for anything left behind before it was time for Jesse to call his cab. It was about two and a half hours to Charleston, but at Jesse's request, I had given him Wyatt's number. Jesse wanted to give the guy an appropriate paycheck for pulling one hell of a favor for us after that first night at dinner, and I didn't mind being spared an awkward few hours in the truck.

"That's great, thanks, Wyatt," Jesse said as he sat on the couch, surrounded by his luggage. "Glad I caught you so close by. See you in a few minutes. I'll be ready."

He hung up the call and smiled up at me anxiously.

"Man," he said, standing up and stretching, "it's going to be hard leaving this house, I've got to say. But I don't like change in general. Guess it's lucky I've managed to stay on the same show for so long," he said, grinning.

I gave a halfhearted nod in reply. After a pause, Jesse pursed his lips, then spoke up again.

"So," he said slowly, "I know we haven't had a chance to talk about it much, but that was...partly because I was hoping I'd have a little more time here," he said. "I wanted to ask if you had any interest in looking for work in L.A.? I've been talking to my agent about tracking down a few people in town who might be looking for personal security soon, once vacation season is over and they start coming back home."

I raised my eyebrows, surprised that he had brought it up now, but I reminded myself it didn't necessarily change anything. It was an offer, but it wasn't concrete. And besides, it wasn't good form to look like I was desperate for a job.

"I appreciate it," I said, trying to use the sincerity in my voice to mask the difficulty I was feeling. "But that's not necessary. Don't feel like you need to go out of your way for me."

"No, I mean it," he said, smiling and taking a few steps closer. "I think L.A. would be a good place for you, if you're interested. It's a world of difference from Winchester, but if you got by all right in Atlanta, you'll love it in the big city."

"Well, didn't say I'd stop you," I said with a soft laugh, and without being asked, I picked up Jesse's bags so that he wouldn't have to rush with it all.

I carried the first two big bags out to the doorstep, but Jesse followed me, and he stopped just behind me in the doorframe.

"Hey," he said, and I paused, setting the bag down and looking over my shoulder at him. "What are – shit," he murmured, and he looked past me at what was coming down the driveway.

Wyatt honked the horn of his cab and waved out the window with a friendly smile on his face, and Jesse frowned as he approached. He looked to me, then back at Wyatt, and he sighed.

"Hold on," he said, and he stormed past me to where Wyatt was pulling up.

I furrowed my brow. Once the cab came to a halt, Jesse leaned in and talked to Wyatt in a tone I couldn't hear. I crossed my arms and watched the cab carefully as Jesse took out his wallet, handed something to Wyatt, then walked back toward me with a resolute look on his face.

Wyatt shrugged at me, waved, and drove away.

"What the hell?" I said, taking a step forward. "Where's he going?"

"To his next job, with the money I had to pay him for the ride to Charleston because I just rebooked it for tomorrow," Jesse said with a serious look on his face.

"What?" I asked, baffled. "Why? Aren't you going to be late to meet with your people?"

"They can wait," Jesse said firmly, "because the whole damn reason I came to Winchester was to get back to a place where I could figure out what was important to me, and just when I think I've got it, I suddenly don't know anymore!"

He reached me, put his hands on my shoulders, and pulled us together for a sudden kiss that made my eyes go wide. It was hungry, fiery, angry, and utterly unexpected. And my body melted in response.

"Marshall," he said after breaking the kiss, glaring at me, "what on earth is going on with you?"

"What's going on with me?" I repeated, blinking. "Look, I'm just trying to make this as easy as it can be, Jesse."

"No, it's more than that," he said insistently, "I know it is. You've been acting strange since you got that call, and I know it's not just me thinking that. Marshall, we've spent almost every hour together since we met. I know when something is up. You're not okay."

He reached for my hand and took it in both of his, and he gave me the most sincere look I had ever seen.

"I don't want to leave you when there's tension between us," he said. "I want to talk about this. For you."

"I don't either," I said, starting to feel the cracks in my armor show. "But you're going to have a lot going on as soon as you get back, Jesse," I said, coming inside and shaking my head.

"Exactly," Jesse said, following me in and shutting the door as I set the bag down. "That's why I want any excuse I can get to have you there with me!"

"You don't have to say that," I insisted, shaking my head again.

"But I do because I care about you, Marshall!" he said, walking around me and cutting off my path to glare at me, and I tensed for a moment.

And then my shoulders relaxed, and I let them slump just a hair. I wasn't about to have an argument with Jesse. I couldn't have, even if I wanted to.

"The call the other night was from my uncle," I finally said, deciding to let it all out at once.

"That's what I was worried about," Jesse said softly, nodding and frowning. "I didn't do it to snoop, but I looked up the company you used to work for. It looked like it had shut down under strange circumstances, but I didn't want to dig up old demons and ask you about it. You're not in trouble, are you? Listen, if he's putting pressure on you, I'll-"

"I'm not in danger," I said, shaking my head. "I... maybe it would make more sense if I explained the whole story."

I nodded for him to follow me, and we headed back out to the porch, where I took a seat on the steps with Jesse and stared out at the tree line long and hard before speaking again.

"My uncle and I go way back," I said. "He was always the one who'd show up and let me skip school to hang out when he blew through town. Mom had complicated feelings about him, but I was just a kid back then. I didn't know better. I was working odd jobs after high school, so when he called me up and said he had an opening at his new nightclub in Atlanta, it was hard to turn that down."

"I bet," Jesse said, watching me carefully. "I would have jumped on that if I had the build for that, too."

"That's about what I told myself," I said. "Started out okay. He was a little sleazier than I had realized, but we got along alright. I learned my job, got good at it, and got paid steadily—at first," I added, frowning. "Over the years, things started fraying. I'd get calls at ass-o'clock in the morning from him asking to get picked up from random places around town. He had a lot of burner phones I had to stop myself from asking about. Eventually, even my paychecks started coming late. I figured that was just what that business was like. Besides, he was family," I added with a sigh.

"That's always a fraught expression," Jesse agreed, nodding.

"With a lot of baggage," I admitted. "About four years ago, I started hearing things from the rest of the staff at the club. I wasn't the only one whose checks were coming late, and if that weren't enough, some of them were talking about getting shorted on tips. The last straw was one morning I was at the club early to make sure some new locks we'd installed were good to go for that night. I happened to be in his office when the phone went off, and I wound up hearing his accountant ranting at me for how my uncle had been dodging him for months. I had no idea what to tell him, so I finally broke down and did some digging on my own."

Jesse watched me with rapt attention as I ran a hand over my face and took a deep breath.

"He was withholding tips and cooking his books," I said. "That was why he was able to pay me as well as he did. I have no idea how much the guy must owe in taxes, but screwing over the other staff was a line I couldn't stomach."

"Oh my god," Jesse breathed. "What did you do?"

"I wanted to confront him and make him give the employees their tips back," I said, remembering how angry and hurt I had felt that night I'd figured it all out. "Hell, I wanted to storm into his apartment and handle it myself, but..." I hesitated. "My uncle was the only guy who had my back in Atlanta. There's a hell of a lot I didn't like about him then and still don't now, but it's hard to shake that. Real hard. Especially since I had been living on that stolen money without knowing it, building up a tidy little savings account and thinking it was all legit."

I shook my head and smiled at my own naivety while Jesse's mouth fell open.

"I didn't want to drag my family name through the mud," I said. "I just kept imagining my mom seeing my uncle and me in the news for something like that, and I just couldn't do that to her. The thought of her having to deal with the town asking her why her son and brother ran off to be a pair of thieves in the big city...I couldn't do it. So I did the next best thing. Without telling my uncle, I packed my bags into my truck and met with some of the senior staff at the club. I passed on all the evidence I'd dug up in a hurry, along with as big a chunk of their backpay as I could from my own savings account. I gave them the number of the best private investigator I knew and suggested they give him a call, and I skipped town. They must have followed through because the club got shut down a few months later after an investigation."

"Holy shit," Jesse said.

"Yeah," I grunted. "'Holy shit' was one of a few things that crossed my mind. I don't know how he isn't in prison, but he's got some new offer on the table for me back in Atlanta."

"You're not thinking about taking it, are you?" Jesse asked, incredulous, but I shrugged.

"Look, Jesse," I said. "We're from different worlds. I'm not letting my past drag you down. You deserve better than that."

"And so do you!" Jesse said, taking my hand as I met his gaze. "Marshall, what you did was downright heroic. Those workers never would have gotten any justice if it hadn't been for you. And you bounced back from that and wound up changing my life in a way I never, ever could have expected. I love you, Marshall," he said, and my heart did a somersault.

"I... fuck, I love you too, Jesse," I said as a wave of emotion unspooled inside me, as if Jesse had pulled a plug and let it all come rushing to the surface.

"You think I don't know that every time we look at each other?" he asked with a soft, meaningful smile as he touched the side of my face. "Your past doesn't dictate your future, Marshall. If you want proof, look at us—you thought you were straight your whole life, and now, we have something that I sure as hell don't want to end. Not tomorrow, not today," Jesse said firmly. "And the future could have something new and beautiful to it because you're *not* your uncle. You're a sweet, thoughtful, wonderful man who just happens to have a damn fine body to match his personality," he said, teasing out a laugh from me. "If that sounds good to you, I mean," he added with a more modest smile.

Jesse and I stared at each other for what felt like an eternity before I finally broke the silence.

"I think," I said, a smile creeping across my lips, as I remembered the episode of *Bannister Heights* that Jesse had tried to start roleplaying with me, "that I have been terribly cruel to you against my better judgment, Adrian Bannister. And I must confess...I've returned to Bannister Heights because I can't keep you off my mind."

JESSE

I COULDN'T KEEP THE EXHILARATED GRIN OFF MY FACE AS I SIGHED happily, folded in Marshall's arms. My heart was racing, adrenaline flooding through my veins as he swept me off my feet and spun me around, pinning me against the front door on the porch of the lake house. His eyes, which had been so sorrowful and cold over the past few days, were bright and shining again. That glorious spark that had captivated me over the weeks I'd spent here with him in this beautiful part of the world had finally returned, and I was over the moon. He leaned in and slowly, softly pressed a kiss to my lips, his hands reaching up to cup my face adoringly. His hard, powerful body rutted and rocked against me as we stood there, entangled in each other's arms, oblivious to the world around us. Nothing mattered more than this moment, this closeness, this man with the watchful eyes and the steady, beautiful heart. And when he started quoting lines of dialogue from Heights back to me, just like I had attempted to do several nights ago, I was so overjoyed I could have melted through the floorboards.

"I never want to be away from you again," he murmured. "Not even for a day."

I smiled against his lips, warming to the roleplay scene.

"There isn't a living soul on this planet or any other who could keep me from you," I whispered back. "No whirling tornado, no stormy sea. No creature great or small. In this life and every single next, I will find you. My heart will find yours in the darkness. I could reach for you with my eyes closed and never miss. We are connected, my light. My hope. My love."

Even though I had memorized these lines months and months ago and recited them with as much feeling as I could muster when we'd filmed the scene, they took on a completely new meaning now that I was saying them to Marshall. Because this time I wasn't playing a part. I wasn't Adrian Bannister. I was Jesse Blackwood, and I was in love.

"Damn, you're one hell of an actor," Marshall laughed softly as he traced his thumb over my bottom lip. I pursed my lips to kiss it with gentle adoration.

Then I shook my head, never breaking eye contact. "I'm not acting this time," I said.

"How can I know for sure?" Marshall asked, and even though he said it playfully, I could see the faint hint of genuine worry in his gorgeous, dark eyes.

"I suppose I'll just have to prove it to you," I replied with a bright smile. "Today. Right now. But also tomorrow and every day that comes after it. I intend to find every way possible to convince you of how I feel. I'll count the ways."

"And how do you feel?" he asked gruffly.

I grinned and dove forward, capturing his lips in an intense, passionate kiss. He moaned softly against my mouth, his hands roving down my body, feeling me up, taking his time. It felt like he was trying to memorize every inch of my frame, commit it all to memory so that he could hold on to it forever, no matter where our paths would take us. When we finally broke apart for a moment, we were both gasping and breathless.

"I feel like a new man," I said, repeating another line from my romantic reunion scene with Beatrice. I knew I'd have to play around with the pronouns a little bit to make it fit, but the sentiment was perfect. "I feel like I've been asleep for years and I had no idea until now. Until you came along. Until you looked at me that very first time and I felt my heart whisper, *there he is; there is the one I have been waiting for.* All this time, I've just been dreaming. I've known you before we even met. My soul knows your soul. We've been together in the stars all along, but now you're here. You're really here, and so am I, and I never want this to end."

Marshall's eyes glimmered as he gazed into mine, a joyous smile growing across his face.

"I'm no Beatrice, but maybe I can still do it justice if I do it my way," he murmured.

With that, he hoisted me up so that I could wrap my legs around his waist, and he reached around to open the front door. We spilled inside, kissing and stroking each other's faces, laughing between kisses.

"No offense to my lovely costar, but I have to say Beatrice ain't got nothing on you," I told him honestly.

"Good. I'm sure she's a great woman, but I would hate to be her competition," he replied, carrying me over to the kitchen and pushing me back to rest on the marble countertop, my legs and arms still wrapped around him.

"They did give her some killer lines, though," I teased.

"Oh, you mean lines like, 'I've been counting down to this moment since the first time you touched me' or 'Every beat of my heart is for you. All of it, everything I am and will ever be, is yours.' Those lines?" Marshall recited perfectly.

My jaw dropped. "Wow. Are you sure you've never done this before?" I asked.

He shrugged. "I've got a good memory. Besides, it feels different saying that stuff when it's… you know, true," he said.

My face flushed as he leaned in to kiss me again, his fingers unbuttoning my shirt and peeling it away. He stepped back for a second to tear off his shirt.

"So you remember the lines," I began, "but what about the love scene? Did you watch that part or did you skip past it?"

"Steamiest PG-13 scene I've ever witnessed in my life," he

remarked. Then he gave me a roguish smirk. "But I bet we can do it better."

He unzipped his jeans and immediately stepped forward to tug my pants down as well, both of us kicking off our shoes. His cock bounced, heavy and thick in the free air, making it difficult for me to focus on anything else. My mouth watered, my fingers itching to touch him. When he moved closer to me, I wrapped my legs around his waist and pulled him tight, trapping him there so I could kiss him while my hands wandered down to wrap around his stiff cock. He groaned into my mouth as I stroked him slowly, almost tantalizing him. I could feel the strength in his body, the restraint he was showing to hold back and resist just taking me right then and there on the kitchen counter. My own cock stiffened, and I wrapped my hands around both our shafts and slid up and down. Marshall's hips involuntarily twitched, and he rocked against me, both of our cocks glistening with beads of precome. His lips traveled down my cheek, down my neck, to breathe softly in my ear. A puff of warm breath near the shell of my ear made me shiver with delight.

"I think you're right," I whispered. "We *can* do it better."

"I've actually thought about this," he said.

"What? Really?" I asked, taken aback.

He smiled and pushed away for a moment, holding up one finger to keep me from trailing after him. He stepped over to the other side of the kitchen and pulled open the junk drawer, which was filled with odds and ends like tape, screws, wood glue, scissors, and extra light bulbs. He rummaged around for a moment or two, then turned around to present a condom and a travel-size bottle of lube. It took all of my willpower not to burst out laughing at the shock.

"Wow. You're prepared, huh?" I chuckled as he walked back over to me, looking awfully damn proud of himself.

"Well, we were messing around a lot upstairs, and I kept thinking, you know, what if we found ourselves ready to go downstairs and then we'd have to go all the way up again... so I just stashed it away here," he said almost sheepishly.

"You're brilliant, you know that?" I said, shaking my head. "Come here."

He growled low in his throat as he stepped back to me, kissing me deeply as he rolled on the condom. He slicked his fingers with lube and began to work me open slowly and carefully, our cocks sliding against each other as we built up the tension higher and higher. I moaned and shivered at the delightful sensation of his fingertips slipping inside me, making my muscles start to loosen up and relax. It wasn't long before he was pressing the head of his cock against my tight hole, his teeth gently grazing my ear as I tensed for the big moment.

"Are you ready?" he murmured gruffly.

I smiled and nodded. "I've been ready since the day we met, Marshall."

"Me, too," he grunted.

He pushed inside of me in one smooth, fluid movement that made my toes curl. I was crunched up on the kitchen counter, my legs swung over Marshall's arms as he braced himself against the wooden cabinets, sliding in and out and striking against my prostate until I was moaning and whimpering, already on the verge of coming.

We rutted together like this, both trying to hold back but losing ourselves to the ebb and flow of incredible shared pleasure. I had never had sex like this before, and with anyone else I might have assumed it was too difficult, too unwieldy. But Marshall was so steady and strong, so measured in every thrust, and so careful to cradle my back perfectly so that the position wasn't painful, that neither one of us could last long. He reared back and slammed into me again and again, every time hitting that delicious spot deep inside me so well, as though he knew precisely how to press my buttons. And I realized with a jolt that it was true—he did know. He had always known, somehow. We just fit together. As unlikely as it had seemed from the start, we were now like one combined presence, moving in perfect tandem, the rhythm getting faster and harder until we were gasping and clutching at one another. Marshall's hips pistoned forward and back a few more times before we clenched up, our bodies tightening as we came together, sighing through our shared release. He pumped into me a few more times as we gasped for air, kissing each other's faces, our fingers interlacing.

"You're right. That was so much better than Beatrice," I said breathlessly.

Marshall laughed, gently pulling out. "Damn straight," he said, then paused and looked thoughtful for a moment. "Although I suppose 'straight' has nothing to do with it."

I couldn't help but laugh as he helped me slide down off the counter. We quickly cleaned up and got dressed again before I realized something.

"Oh! I left my suitcases out front," I said, blushing. "I guess we should go get them."

"Right. As if anyone could get past the perimeter to take them," Marshall boasted.

But we walked hand in hand out to the front porch, both drifting on cloud nine. We each grabbed a suitcase and then paused to kiss on the porch before going inside. We were so distracted with bliss, in fact, that when we heard the snap-flash of a camera lens, it took us a few seconds to recognize the awful sound.

"What the hell was that?" Marshall snarled, looking around angrily.

"Shit. How could that be possible?" I murmured.

We both looked around until my eyes clocked the swiftly moving man darting away through the trees. Marshall scowled with rage, and his hands curled into fists as he jumped off the porch to chase after the guy.

"I'll kick his ass!" he bellowed, and I had no doubt he would.

But then something oddly comforting occurred to me.

"Wait!" I called out to him, and Marshall whipped around, looking confused. I gave him a reassuring shrug and a smile. "Just let him go."

"What? Why?" he said.

"I don't care anymore. If he wants to print a photo of us kissing, he can be my guest. I don't give a damn. I'm not ashamed, Marshall. I'm proud. I'm okay with it if you are," I said.

Marshall's scowl melted into a grin, and he jogged back up to the porch to kiss me.

When we broke apart, he gazed deep into my eyes.

"I'm more than okay with it, Jesse," he said softly. "I've fallen for you."

"And I'm head over heels for you," I replied.

"Good," Marshall said. "Because I'm not done with you yet."

He scooped me up and carried me back inside for round two.

And we didn't care who saw.

MARSHALL

THE MONTHS REALLY FLY BY IN LOS ANGELES, EVEN MORE SO WHEN you're keeping busy. And if there was one thing Jesse and I had both been these past few months, it was busy, in every possible way.

I stood up from the conference table I was sitting at, and I stepped around it to shake the hand of the man I had just interviewed for my new security company. In the first month of moving to L.A. with Jesse, I had become the founder and owner of Hawkins Security Solutions, and thanks to Jesse's connections, I was off to a roaring start with a healthy list of star-studded clients who had a glowing recommendation from Jesse himself.

"Thanks for your time, Max," I said, giving him a firm handshake as he gave me a gruff smile. "I'll review everything I've got on file for you now and get back to you by the end of the week."

"Thank you, Mr. Hawkins," he said with a professional nod before he picked up his folder and gathered his papers in short order. "Should I touch base in a few days and see if there's anything else you'll need?"

"Feel free," I said. "Looking forward to it. Here, let me walk you to the elevator."

Max was a no-brainer. I honestly could have hired him right then and there with a relatively clean conscience. He was former military with a few years' experience in private security under his belt already, and his body was every bit as well suited to this line of work as mine was. The guy had an intensity in his eyes that I half-jokingly thought would do half the security work for him.

But I knew the value of background checks better than anyone else, so I forced myself to stick to my rule of never offering a job without a thorough check. If there was anything to talk about in the past, I liked to talk about it and hear their side of the story. I figured that was only fair, considering my personal track record, and it had served me well so far.

I gave Max a nod as the metal doors of the elevator closed between us, and I smiled as I checked my to-do list. That was the last interview of the day, and it had been one hell of a long day. Max was just one of several of these human powerhouses who had shown up to apply for a job in my company, and I had a feeling I'd be hiring at least three of the guys I interviewed today.

This was going better than I could have possibly hoped for, and I had Jesse to thank for it.

The one part of living in L.A. that I hadn't adapted well to was the traffic, so it was well after dark before I finally got home to Jesse's apartment, where I had gladly moved in after our last day in Winchester together. But as I had told my mom, it was only a temporary last day.

I flew to Winchester to visit Mom at every chance I got. Jesse had even gone out of his way last month to bring her to the studio and let her meet all the cast of the show. She still had stars in her eyes by the time she'd gotten back to Winchester, and the rest of Jesse's colleagues had my undying affection for being so welcoming to her.

What Mom didn't know was that I had been quietly looking for openings for experienced electricians in our area. I had a feeling she was more than happy to stay put in Winchester, but Jesse and I both thought it would be nice to at least make the offer. Besides, it would probably put my mom's mind at ease, knowing I lived somewhere I felt happy inviting her. This was not round two of Atlanta, and I wanted that to be abundantly clear.

I stepped into the apartment to the delicious smell of falafel being cooked, and I gave an audible sigh of delight as I kicked off my shoes and went into the kitchen to find Jesse. He looked over his shoulder to grin at me and waggle his eyebrows as I approached him from behind and hugged him around the waist, peering down at the sizzling fried chickpea patties in the skillet.

"You're getting better at handling traffic," Jesse said, pushing his butt back into me idly. "Here I was hoping to have this ready by the time you got home."

"I'll just have to snack on something else while I wait," I growled, kissing him on the neck and nipping at it just enough to get those goose bumps I liked feeling.

"Oh no!" He played along. "Damn, if only I had a bodyguard to help me through trying times like this..."

I laughed and squeezed his ass before making my way to the cabinets and mixing us a couple of gin and tonics. They had grown on us over the months, especially after experimenting with different tonic waters and taking liberties with adding more lemon and lime to the mix. Jesse had managed to not only maintain his new figure but make it look even more fit, and I couldn't have been more proud of him for achieving his goals.

"I think we deserve a toast," I said, walking Jesse's drink over to him after he pulled the last of the falafel out of the skillet and set it to dry on the plate of paper towels.

"Well, with my skills, this falafel probably doubles as toast," Jesse murmured, but he took the glass and kissed me on the cheek before holding it up. "But I couldn't agree more. To the new house!"

We clinked our glasses together and drank... to the lake house in Winchester we had just put a down payment on. Jesse had sent me an email this morning after we had gone our separate ways for work, letting me know it had gone through, and the sale was definitely going to be a reality.

Jesse's new season of *Bannister Heights* had come with a few new sponsors that amounted to a generous signing bonus, and we couldn't think of a more fitting way to christen our new life together than putting it to use on something we'd both get a lot of use out of. The owner of the lake house didn't even live in Winchester anymore and was happy to part with it, and it meant we would have a vacation house to go to whenever we wanted to visit my hometown and unwind in the great outdoors.

We didn't even sit down at the table to eat dinner. We just ate while sitting on the counters of the kitchen and talking excitedly about what kinds of things we wanted to decorate the place with. Jesse had a vibrant vision for the place, and since I knew my minimalist tastes were in need of freshening up, I was warming up to a few different design choices that were outside my comfort zone.

As we did the dishes together afterward, I filled Jesse in on my interviews at work, and he talked to me about how the day had been on set—which was more or less how most of our evenings went nowadays. It couldn't have been more ideal, if you asked me.

"Now that you mention it, that reminds me," Jesse said as we dried off our hands, "my agent was talking about needing to hire security for a gala the producers for the show are holding at the end of the month. Might be a good way to make some friends if you aren't booked up already. I warned him your hires won't be able to compare to you, but he said he didn't expect me to say otherwise."

"Flattering," I said, grinning, "but no, 'not as good as Marshall' probably isn't a great slogan for my employees."

"Well, it's true for me, at least," he said, smirking as I took hold of his hips and swayed from side to side playfully.

"That's all right," I said. "I'm the only one who'll be protecting you, anyway, so long as you're in arm's reach of me."

"That's where I like to be," he said with lidded eyes.

I smiled as I let him turn me around so that I was the one against the counter, and after a quick kiss on the lips, he sank to his knees and looked up at me with nothing but pure, unfiltered love in his eyes. We had other evening traditions that were a little less appropriate for polite conversation, but when we were fresh from talking about the house and the life we had on the horizon, it was hard to resist.

He unbuttoned my pants in a matter of seconds, spurred on by the sight of my thick cock outlined so clearly just under the surface of the fabric. He freed it with one hand and pressed a kiss to it as if it were a dear friend he had missed, and his tongue came next.

I gripped the counter's edge and let my head fall back softly as he pressed warm, wet kisses to my hardened shaft as I spoke. "I've been thinking about this since I kissed you goodbye this morning," I growled. "My cock kept getting hard when I was alone at the office."

"Glad I'm not the only one," he murmured as my cock slid against his cheek, and he kissed my balls. "God, I can't wait to get you working at the studio again."

"They'll catch us if we're not careful," I warned him playfully, running my hands through his hair.

"I don't care," he said. "Let them."

"That's what I like to hear," I said, and I felt him take my bulging crown into his mouth.

At first, he lavished the tip with attention, using his hand to pump my shaft and his other to massage my balls. They were always heavy for him, always waiting impatiently for the next time I could release them with Jesse. He took up my every steamy thought and made my heart beat faster every time I thought of him, which was so often that I felt like I'd be in shape no matter what we decided to cook in this sinful kitchen of ours.

Jesse's tongue found the edge of my crown and worked its way around it, pushing against every soft surface it could find. He was a tease, and it was leading up to the long, powerful strokes he gave the lower half of my manhood a moment later. I groaned freely as the warm ripples of sensation started moving up my body. My muscles craved this release every day. Jesse was my vice, my reward, and my love. And every day we spent together only fanned those flames hotter.

He got faster and faster, taking almost my entire cock into his mouth. He felt my body's subtle changes as he brought me closer to the edge every time those soft pink lips slid down the girth of my cock. His eyes looked up at me in adoration, and I couldn't keep a grin off my face as I looked down and caressed him.

Then I felt white-hot sensation shoot through me, and I knew I was close. Jesse tasted my precome, and he worked me to the final stretch. He didn't hold back, sucking my aching cock with everything he had, back and forth in a perfect rhythm.

Finally, I clenched my fists in his hair like he'd asked me to so often in bed, and I toppled over the edge of my orgasm. My balls tightened, and I shot thick, heavy release into Jesse, which he took in with hungry, lustful moans.

He slid off my cock with a soft pop and stood up slowly, where I wrapped him in my arms and peppered him with kisses. We stood there, listening to each other's heartbeat for a few moments, enjoying each other's silent company.

This was my life, as much as I couldn't believe it, and I was going to hold it so tight that I'd never let go.

Jesse's phone buzzed on the counter, snapping us out of the moment. He smiled and pecked me on the cheek, then went to check it.

"Don't get too wrapped up in a work call," I warned him with a smile. "It's your turn next, and I'm finishing you off in the shower," I informed him.

"It's not a work email, actually," he said, eyebrows shooting up as a smile spread across his face as he looked up at me and showed me the email. "It's an invitation to Carter and Mark's wedding back in Winchester—and they want you to be a groomsman!"

THE END

ALSO BY JASON COLLINS

Worth the Weight Series:

Weight for Love (Worth the Weight Book 1)

Hard Tackle (Worth the Weight Book 2)

The Bodyguard (Worth the Weight Book 3)

Standalone Novels:

His Submissive

Protecting the Billionaire

The Weight is Over

The Boyfriend Contract

Chasing Heat

Dom

Weight for Happiness

Straight by Day

Raising Rachel

The Warehouse

The Jewel of Colorado

Love & Lust

Forbidden

72890570R00112

Made in the USA
Columbia, SC
01 September 2019